MY BROTHER'S STORY

MY BROTHER'S STORY

Allen Johnson Jr.

Illustrated by Kelley McMorris

MY BROTHER'S STORY by Allen Johnson Jr.

© 2014 Allen Johnson Jr.

Published by PREMIUM PRESS AMERICA

ISBN 978-1-933725-37-6
Library of Congress Catalog Card Number 2013915241

Blackwater Novels are available at special discounts for premiums, sales promotions, fundraising, or educational use. For details contact the publisher at P.O. Box 58995, Nashville TN 37205-8995; or phone toll-free 800-891-7323, or 615-353-7902, or fax 615-353-7905, or go to www.premiumpressamerica.com.

To contact the author, write or call the publisher or go to www.blackwaternovels.com

Illustrations by Kelley McMorris, Kelley McMorris Illustration

Cover and interior design by Sara L. Chapman, Art Squad Graphics

Printed in the United States of America

10   9   8   7   6   5   4   3   2   1

Dedicated to the memory of my grandfather,

P.G. Shook

Introduction

Allen Johnson Jr. is persistent.

He never gives up, and unlike most of us, he just keeps on ticking away at the storyteller's craft.

He's at his best in *My Brother's Story*.

This lively, witty, and real-feeling tale of twin brothers living in parallel universes in the always-old Old South will gently get under your skin and make its way into your heart.

Allen speaks from experiential memory—that's why you tend to forget that you're *reading*. Your senses awaken. You can smell the pine trees and honeysuckle, hear the relentless critters in the swamp, and feel the Blackwater River flowing by under a star-blended sky.

You start to feel your way through the pages. By the time you run smack into the last line of the last chapter, you want to continue anyhow. You wonder, *What happens the next day? And the next...?*

Savor the moment. You might not read any evocation of childhood that's this much fun for a long time to come.

Jim Reed — writer, bookseller, film actor and lover of good books

Chapter One

Johnny

SUMMERTIME, WHEN I laid in bed, and it was too hot to sleep, that train running up the valley was a heap of comfort to me. I weren't allowed to have no light, and with the bugs chirrin' or some old owl hooting, it got mighty scary. The railroad tracks come right up the valley, and, laying in that bed, I know'd that sooner or later a train would be along. I'd hear one chuffin' up the grade long before I could see the light. It would sound so friendly and interesting that I would forget about being scared.

Sometimes in the morning I would sneak out early and follow a game trail down to the tracks to see the Birmingham train pull in and take on water. That's how I come to be settin' up on the bank by the railroad tracks that morning. I know'd where the train stopped to take on water, and I had me a spot on the bank where I could watch her real good.

That morning, I'd woke up early from the dream. It was something I dreamed a lot...about my mother...and it always made me feel sad and happy at the same time. It was a confusing dream. I'd be layin' on a quilt with picnic stuff all around me, and I'd look up and, even though I was still on the quilt, I'd see Momma walking through the grass leading me by the hand.

Her hair was all gold-looking, but she'd be turned away so I couldn't see her face. She'd call, Come on, Johnny! and start to turn my way, but before I could see her face real clear, I'd always wake up.

So this dream had woke me up, and I snuck out real early even though it meant getting no breakfast. I had me a cold biscuit left from some Sarah had give me the night before when Aunt Min had sent me to bed without no supper. I had messed up again for sure and spilt a glass of milk when I set down at the table. Auntie took me outside and whipped on my legs with a switch. It hurt enough, but I was used to it and never made no sound. This made her madder. She whipped harder, and I pulled my breath in through my teeth. I weren't goin' to give her the pleasure of making me holler.

Uncle Joe was a preacher and used to preach hell fire and damnation in his church every Sunday. He was a big, strong man with great big hands, but around Aunt Min, he kind of shrunk up and got mild as cow's milk. Once when she was goin' to whip me for tracking dirt in the house, he tried to stick up for me, but she tongue-lashed him so hard that he slunk off to the back yard looking worse than me, and I was some miserable.

Anyway, the Birmingham passenger train used to come through the valley about six every morning, but that day it was late. The sun come up and I stretched back against a tree, rubbing the switch marks on the back of my legs and picking at a callus on the bottom of my foot near my little toe, wondering what it would be like to have a real home. I remember I got up and peed off the bank on a toad that was down near the tracks and then laid back down.

The sun felt real good, and I laid there smelling some honeysuckle and went plumb to sleep on that red clay bank like it was a feather bed. The engine was almost at me when I popped awake, feeling excited like I always did when I seen a train. The bell was clanging, and the engine was hissing out steam, and I scooted over to the edge of the bank to get a better look and laid down, propped up on my elbows. The Birmingham train chunked to a stop, and I was staring into a Pullman car at a boy who was sitting on a bed rubbing his eyes. He took his hands down, and I near about fell off the bank. That boy had red hair and freckles, and his ears stuck out. He had a gap in his front teeth. He looked at me, and his eyes got big. I reckon mine did, too. 'Cept for not being skinny, that boy was me.

It was the summer of 1937. School was out for the year, which weren't so good for me. Most of the fun I had was at school. If I wanted to have fun in the summer, I had to sneak out of the house real early and stay out. Aunt Min would lay into me every time I done this, but she usually whipped me anyway, so I didn't have nothing to lose.

After the Birmingham train pulled out, I went to a swimming hole I know'd about on the creek. I just lazed around and chucked rocks at frogs and one old water moccasin I seen goin' up the bank. When I run out of rocks, it had got pretty hot, so I pulled off my clothes and slid in the water and floated on my back. After a while, I climbed out and layed in the sun on a big patch of rock to get dry and thought about that boy I seen on the train.

Long about lunchtime I was hungry, and then I remembered it was Friday, which was the day Aunt Min went to her bible study group at the church. She never got home 'til suppertime on Friday, so I figured I'd go on back and get some grub from Sarah, and I did. She heated up some black-eyed peas for me and give me some country ham and a big hunk of cornbread with a glass of buttermilk. After I put that away, I felt some better and told her I'd help her churn the butter.

We was settin' on the little screen porch behind the kitchen, and when I took the churn handle, Sarah got up and moved to the other chair by the porch table. She pulled her feet out of her shoes and flexed her toes. Her stockings was rolled down below her knees.

"Law, these ol' feets git tired, and I ain't even started to cook dinner yet."

"Sarah," I said, "something really funny happened this morning." I told her about the train and the boy on it who had looked at me.

"My, my, my!" Sarah shook her head. "If that don't beat

all." She pursed her mouth and looked at me hard, studying on something. "Honey, I'm goin' to tell you something I ain't even 'sposed to know."

She bent over and put her head in her hands and her elbows on her knees. "You know yo' momma and daddy got killed in a automobile accident? Well, one night, after you been here just a few months—you still wasn't three years old —I was 'bout to come in to clear the table after dinner when I heard yo' aunt giving Mister Joe the devil. She say: 'Both of 'em?! 'Course we couldn't have took both of 'em! I don't even want the one we got!' She was talking 'bout you, honey. I'm sorry, but that's what she say."

"It don't matter none," I told Sarah. "I always know'd she didn't want me. She ain't never hugged me or nothing. She don't even like me."

Sarah looked at me and her eyes was shining.

"Well," she went on, "I stopped and stood real still right there by the kitchen door, and I heard Mr. Joe say: 'If you don't want the boy, Minnie, why did you take him in?' Then she say: 'It was my Christian duty to take in my sister's child. How was I to know he would be such a troublesome boy.'

"'But little Will yo' sister's chile, too, Minnie,' Mr. Joe say. 'If you didn't want both boys, you should have let Johnny go to Birmingham with them Jennisons. They wanted to take both of 'em, and twins ought to stay together.'

"I never heard Mr. Joe so brave, but it didn't do him no good. 'You get out of my house, Joe Brasher!' she say, real mean-sounding, 'You get quick, or you goin' to wish you had!' That's what I heard, honey. That other chile's name is Will, and, according to Mr. Joe, he went to Birmingham to some folks called Jennison. It seem mighty funny, but maybe that boy you seen today…well, maybe he was yo' twin brother…"

All of a sudden I understood that dream I'd been having. It weren't me my mother was leading through the grass. It was my brother. I quit working that churn. Sarah, she grabbed me and give me a long, hard hug. Then she run her hands down my side, feeling my ribs.

"Honey," she said, "you just skin and bone. What with putting you to bed without no supper most every night, that woman gone starve you to death."

"Not as long as you're here, Sarah," I says. I felt stronger from the food and started to slosh that churn up and down with a will.

"Tha's right, Johnny," she says, "but yo' aunt goin' to catch me sneaking you food one day, and when she do, she turn me loose. She fire me just as sure as I'm settin' here. Yo' aunt think I can't get work if she fire me. Shoot! There's two ladies just waiting for Sarah to come cook for 'em. Nice ladies, too. I can pick and choose where I work."

"Why ain't you left already," I says, but I already know'd the answer.

"You, honey. Nothin' keeping me here but you."

"Sarah, if you was to leave here, I would, too," I told her. Sarah looked worried.

"Where you think you be goin'? I can't take you in. Yo' aunt wouldn't stand for it."

A fly lit on my knee. I quit churning and eased my hand up to my knee and made a grab right over the fly so it flew right into my hand. I threw it against the window pane, and it made a little blip sound and fell back on the table, knocked goofy and buzzin' around in circles on its back. Sarah grabbed the fly swatter and put an end to it.

"If you was to leave, where you think you be goin'?" she asked me again.

"Birmingham," I told her.

Chapter Two

Will

I WAS WALKING ACROSS a grassy field with Momma. She held my hand and when I looked up at her, she was real pretty with lots of blond hair around her face. I looked back and saw myself lying on a quilt next to a picnic basket, and Momma called out: 'Come on, Johnny.' I said: 'I'm Will, Momma. I'm right here!' and looked at her again and her hair had turned to red, and now she was my new mother....

The train stopped with a jerk that yanked me out of my dream. Sunlight was coming under the window shade, shining in on my lower berth, and I got real excited 'cause I remembered I was on the train.

Daddy was a vice president of the L&N railroad, and sometimes he took Momma and me on his business trips. I used to love to go because riding on a train is just about the most fun and exciting thing in the whole world. We were on our way back to Birmingham from Cincinnati on the Pan American. It was a good train and I was enjoying every minute of it.

I pinched together the two metal tabs on the shade, and

pushed it up. The light was dazzley, but I saw a red clay bank like we have in the South. I rubbed my eyes and looked again, and up on the bank lying in the grass there was a boy looking at me. I've never been so surprised. The boy had red hair and a gap in his teeth. He had freckles and his ears stuck out. He was dirty and skinny, but, except for that, he was the spitting image of me! We locked eyes, and the train rolled out. I put my cheek on the window to watch him as long as I could.

"Will? You up?" Daddy whispered, slapping on the dark green curtain that closed in the lower berth.

"Yes, sir."

"Your mother's still asleep in the compartment. Meet me in the dining car. We'll have breakfast."

"OK, Daddy," I said, grabbing my clothes out of the little net hammock over the windows. "Be there in a minute." I pulled on my shorts and my shirt and shoes and socks and unbuttoned the prickly green curtain. I climbed out of my berth and headed for the men's room. There was a curtain hanging over the men's room door, and I pushed it aside and went in. It smelled like tobacco smoke, disinfectant, metal, and leather. James, the porter, was sitting there on the black leather seat polishing the spittoon. He put it down and began to button up his white coat.

"Morning, Will," he said. "Your daddy was just in here. Mister Frank don't sleep too late when he travel."

Since Daddy was a vice president of the railroad, most of the men who worked on the trains knew him. When he traveled with Momma, they always had the sleeping compartment at the end of the car.

"Morning, James. Yeah, Daddy likes to be the first one in the dining car." I ran some water in the shiny, metal sink, splashed my face and dried off with one of the white and blue towels, then I went in the little room where the toilet was. When I stepped on the foot pedal, the bottom of the toilet flipped down, and you could see the crossties whooshing by under the train with a fine lot of noise. It gave me a straight shot onto the rail bed. When I came out of the little room, I said:

"James, do you know where that last stop was?"

"That was just a water stop. 'Bout ten mile north of Columbia, Tennessee. We be coming into Columbia in a few minutes."

I had to go through two coach cars to get to the diner and they were pretty full; mostly colored folks still trying to sleep.

They didn't look too comfortable. I felt guilty that I had a lower berth, while the colored people had to sit up all night. The cars smelled like hair oil and cheap perfume. The train was goin' fast for such a rough roadbed, and I had to grab the tops of the seats to keep from landing in somebody's lap. I threw my shoulder against the heavy metal door to push it open, and this blast of noise hit me. I kind of tippytoed across the steel plates that were sliding and moving around between the cars.

The dining car steward was a white man who wore a dark blue uniform. He was like a headwaiter, and he took me to Daddy's table. As usual, Daddy was neat and well dressed; just shaved and wearing a gray suit with a vest and a tie. He had wavy brown hair and a warm smile that showed up in his eyes. His nose was long and everybody said he looked English, which he probably did since all of his great grandparents came from England.

"Morning, son. Hungry?"

"Yes, sir," I said, sliding into the chair across from him next to the window. The train was slowing as it pulled into Columbia. I could hear a crossing bell getting louder and louder. The town was still asleep, but there was an old flatbed truck stopped at the crossing. A farmer in blue coveralls had got out of the truck and was leaning on the open door watching the train go by. There was an old hound on the flatbed and, as we rolled by, I saw the farmer bend over to spit tobacco juice. The clanging bell died down as we passed. Looking out of a train is about the most interesting thing you can do, but I couldn't keep my mind on what I was looking at.

"That's a rough stretch of tracks north of Columbia," Daddy said as the waiter came up with our grapefruit juice. "Bet it woke your mother up." He turned to the waiter. "John, take Mrs. Jennison some orange juice, toast and coffee when you have time, will you please? We're in the compartment in car G-30."

"Yes, suh, Mister Frank. Glad to," he said, putting down my juice and moving aside silverware and glasses to spread a white napkin over a wet spot on the tablecloth. "Stuff always spill when we coming through here."

"We're goin' to do some work on this stretch of tracks in a few months, John."

"Sho glad to hear it, Mister Frank. Save us a heap of napkins." John went to the kitchen and came back with a tray full of food, and me and Daddy tucked into our eggs and bacon. They tasted smoky and greasy and delicious. I kept thinking about that boy. We finished eating, and Daddy was sipping his coffee. He lit up his pipe.

"You're mighty quiet, son. What's on your mind?" Daddy asked me.

"Daddy, something happened this morning back there at that water stop." I told him about the boy. "He looked so much like me, Daddy, it was like I was looking at myself. It was strange. I can't stop thinking about him."

Daddy rubbed his chin with his thumb and forefinger and kind of chewed on his lower lip. He just looked at me for a long time, then he said:

"Tell you what, Will, let's go on back to the compartment and tell your mother about that boy."

Momma was sitting on the lower berth with Daddy's robe on, drinking coffee and looking out the window.

"Morning, sweetie," she said, giving me a hug and a kiss on the cheek. "You, too, big sweetie," she said, grinning at Daddy. She patted the berth, and I climbed up at her feet. Daddy sat on the little bench across from the berth.

Momma's hair was dark red like mine, so that it looked like I really was her natural son. She wasn't funny-looking like me, though, with sticking-out ears and freckles. She was beautiful, but that's not all...she was fun. She had a deep down laugh and could sing and play the piano better than anybody. She did have a hot temper. Once in a while she and Daddy would have an argument which would usually end with her cussing and throwing something at him. I tried to stay out of the way when that happened.

"Honey," Daddy said, "something funny happened to Will this morning. Not funny 'ha-ha,' funny 'strange.' Tell your mother about it, Will."

When I finished, Momma and Daddy just looked at each other.

"Seems like an awful coincidence," Momma said. "Yeah, but it fits, Allie. The Brashers live near Columbia. We have to tell Will the whole story."

"Yes, we do," said Momma. "It's time he knew, anyway."

She looked at me for a while and then reached out and took my hand in both of hers. "Honey, you know your real parents were killed in an automobile accident?"

"Yes, ma'am."

"Well, honey, you had a brother...a twin. We tried to get both of you, but your real mother's sister insisted on taking your brother. She lived somewhere up near Columbia, Tennessee."

"His name was Johnny," I said.

"How'd you know that?" Daddy asked me.

"I have this dream about him. I have it over and over. I didn't understand it 'til now. My first Momma calls him Johnny in the dream. Then she turns into you," I said looking at Momma. We all just sat there for a while, as the train rolled through some woods and then broke out into farm country. There were cows grazing. They didn't even look up. The train started around a long bend, and I could see the engine ahead putting out lots of smoke. "That boy...he didn't look too good," I said. "He was dirty and sort of skinny."

"Frank,..." Momma said. Daddy leaned back staring out the window. He was chewing his lip again, then he turned to me.

"Will, next week I have to go up to Columbia on business. You come with me. We'll ask around some, maybe check at the court house. I know the last name. It's Brasher. We ought to be able to find where they live. I want to check on that boy. See how he's doing. You want to meet your brother?"

"Yes sir," I said. "I want that a whole lot."

Chapter Three

Johnny

WELL, AUNT MIN DIDN'T catch Sarah giving me food, but she found out about it. It was my fault, too, but I don't feel bad about it. Getting Sarah fired from working for Aunt Min was the best thing I ever done for her.

What happened was, I was in bed with no supper again. Same old thing. I don't know what I done. I think I left some smudges on the piano keys. Anyway, Sarah had brung me some cornbread with melted butter on it, and I dropped some crumbs in the bed. Aunt Min found them the next day and fired Sarah. I remember she was screeching at Sarah something awful. She told her she hadn't sent me to bed with no supper to have somebody sneaking behind her back and feeding me.

"Miz Brasher, somebody got to feed this boy, or you goin' to kill him," Sarah told her. "Boys got to eat. If I didn't feed this chile, he be starved, the way you do him."

"You're fired!" Aunt Min screeched. "Git out of this house! I won't have no useless nigger tellin' me what to do. Don't expect no reference neither. You'll never get another job. Not if I can help it!"

"Miz Brasher, I done already got another job. Twice the money, too. I'm goin' to Miz Barncastle and thankful of it. I had 'bout all I can stand of workin' in this house. Lord help this boy without me here to feed him."

Aunt Min was spluttering and starting to use words that a preacher's wife ain't even supposed to know, but Sarah wouldn't talk no more. She just looked at Auntie like she was some kind of disgusting bug and turned around and left the room.

I snuck outside and cut through the woods and waited on the dirt road to Carter's Creek, which was where Sarah lived. Pretty soon I seen her walking up the road.

"Hey, Sarah," I said. When she saw me by the fence she come over, and we hugged each other.

"Sarah sho goin' to miss you, honey," she told me. Her eyes were shining, and mine felt kind of full-up, too.

"Sarah," I said, "someday when I got a lot of money, I'm goin' to come back and get you. You can work for me, and I'll pay you lots of money... all you need."

"I knows you will, honey, but just now, Sarah wants to give you something." She reached into the pocket of her dress and pulled out a change purse and unsnapped it. She took out some money, took a rubber band off it and pulled off five one-dollar bills. She pushed 'em down in my shirt pocket. "Johnny, if you goin' to try to get to Birmingham, you need to have some money with you. Hide this real good. Don't let nobody know you got it, and, honey, if you goin' to try to get away, wait 'til your aunt and uncle goes away for a spell, so you gets a good start. If you don't, they goin' to catch you for sure."

"I can't take your money, Sarah," I told her. "You need your money."

I got enough, honey, and I got a good job now. You pay Sarah back when you rich."

"I will, Sarah. I promise I will."

"Johnny," she took hold of my hands, "you be real careful of grown up folks 'til you get somewhere safe. They some bad grown-ups. Some of 'em worse than your aunt." She turned me lose, clamped her mouth tight and started up the road.

"I will be careful, Sarah..."

Not having Sarah around was bad, but eating Aunt Min's cooking made it worse. After a few days, I was beginning to think I'd rather starve, then I got lucky. Thursday afternoon, Aunt Min told me they was goin' to Columbia the next day to a revival meeting. They wouldn't be back 'til late on Sunday. She needed me to stay home and feed the chickens and the pig. Said there was peanut butter and bread and canned soup that I could fix to eat. She said that if I broke anything or got anything dirty, she'd have the hide off of me. She told me she didn't trust me, but didn't have no choice 'cause there weren't no one else to look after the farm. I was wondering how you could call ten broke-down acres, half-covered in kudzu, a "farm" when there weren't no more to it than a few falling down sheds and an old house; but I just kept saying "yes'm," "yes'm," over and over. I was tickled pink that they was leaving.

Late that afternoon, after they'd gone, I started getting ready to leave. It felt kind of spooky wandering around that old house alone. It weren't no home, but it was the only place I'd lived, and the thought of leaving was scary. I got some tee

shirts and a pair of short pants and some socks and rolled all
that up in the blanket off my bed and tied it up with some
rope. Then I got me a paper bag of food ready: some peanut
butter-and-jelly sandwiches, some slices of ham, and some
crackers. I put the pocket knife that Uncle Joe had give me
on the sly in one pocket and a couple of boxes of matches in
the other. I folded the five one-dollar bills flat, wrapped them
in waxed paper, got a big safety pin out of Aunt Min's sewing
basket and pinned the money inside my overalls. I put out
extra food and water for the chickens, fed the pig and turned
him lose so he could root around. 'Bout then I heard thunder.
The air had got real still, and the sky was dark. I went up
to the attic where my little bedroom was and looked out the
attic window. I could see a big thunderstorm moving up the
valley. The attic got darker. Lightning struck all around the
end of the valley. Thunder rolled my way, and a gust of cool,
wet wind whuffed against the house. I watched the storm
build. Lightning struck real close in the woods with a wonderful crack, and the trees started to toss like crazy. Rain
come in sheets, and then it started to hail. Hail stones big
as hickory nuts rattled off the tin roof and rolled around the
yard. It was over quick as it started. The afternoon sun come
in under the clouds and everything smelled wet and steamy.
I'd been scared about running away, but the storm fixed that.
Now I was excited and itching to get started. Even though
I wasn't scared no more, I still wanted to get down to the
tracks before dark. I didn't want to go through them woods
in the pitch dark.

I wrote a note for aunt Min. It said: *"I'm leaving and ain't
coming back. Say goodbye to Uncle Joe. I know he would
have been nice to me if he weren't scared to. Johnny."* I got my

blanket roll and the paper bag and went on out to the game trail that led down to the tracks. I went to the spot where I had always watched the trains stop for water. I had me a long wait. The light turned all blue and purple, and the lightning bugs come out. Before I know'd it, I couldn't see my hand in front of my face, but after a time, the moon come up. Even with the moon, it was pretty spooky settin' out there with the bugs singing and two owls talking to each other in the woods.

It must have been about after eleven when a freight train finally come. With the full moon hanging over the woods, I could see pretty good. The engine stopped at the water tank, and I slid down the bank and walked back along the cars. There was mostly cars full of coal and tank cars. There was only three boxcars and two of them were locked up and sealed. The door on the third boxcar was slid open a few inches. I pulled it open some more and tried to see in but couldn't see nothing. I had never got on no freight train before, and my heart was knocking.

"Here goes," I says. I threw my stuff in and pulled myself up and rolled onto the floor of the car. After a minute, I slid the door mostly shut and struck a match. There weren't nothing there but sacks of feed stacked up in one end of the car. I climbed up on 'em and started to shift 'em around 'til I had me a kind of trench near the back of the car. I had heard that the railroad police sometimes checked boxcars for hobos and would put you in jail if you were caught, so I wanted to be hid. Then I tossed my stuff up on the feed sacks and got settled in the trench I had made. It was black as sin in that car, but I know'd I could open the door when the train started and let in some moonlight. The sacks of feed weren't no feather bed, but not too bad.

It was a warm night, so I used my blanket roll for a pillow and stretched out and started munching some of the crackers out of my paper bag. The train give a jerk and started to roll. Soon we was clicking along at a good clip. I was more excited than ever and climbed down and slid the door open a couple of feet. I set on the edge of the car, dangling my legs down and smelling the night air. Farm fields and woods and thickets covered with kudzu slid by in the moonlight. It was beautiful. The breeze was taking the smoke away, but once we went around a bend and the smoke come back over the train, and I near 'bout choked. Got a cinder in my eye, too, but that weren't nothing. I pulled my eyelid over the bottom one and got it out like you would a gnat.

I was feeling real cocky to be riding along like I was 'til something cut the bottom out from under me. The train eased onto a siding to let another train by, and as it stopped, I was looking down a bank at a little white house. It weren't thirty feet from the tracks. I could see right in the house. I seen a lady in a long white nightgown carry a candle into a small room and put it down next to a bed where a little girl was tucked up. The woman set down on the bed and patted the child and leaned over and kissed her. The little girl reached up and put her arms around the woman's neck and hugged her real hard. Well, sir, it done something to me. I climbed back up on those sacks and sat there with my fists clenched and my teeth clenched, but sobs started coming out of my chest, and I couldn't stop 'em, and I laid down and cried like I was a little boy. The train started up again, and I was still crying but after a while, I 'bout got it stopped. Every once in a while a big old sob would come up. The motion of the train and the clicking of the wheels on the track was peaceful, though, and I must have gone to sleep.

When the train jerked to a stop, I woke up. I heard voices. Men walking back along the train.

"Hey Ed, this here car's wide open. Wait up 'til I check it out."

A light flashed around the car, and I hunkered down amongst the feed sacks.

"Nobody here." The door slid shut. I heard some rattling sound at the end of the car like it was being unhooked, then nothing for a long while. I was just dozing off when something slammed into the car. Then we was rolling again and slamming into other cars, jerking this way and that way. Every time I'd start to go to sleep, we'd bang into something else. Finally the slam-banging stopped and, we were moving again. After a while, when I felt sure we was out in the country, I slid the door open. I could see some light in the sky and know'd it was almost dawn.

"Oh, Lord!" I said out loud. I weren't headed towards Birmingham. The train was goin' in the other direction.

Chapter Four

Will

*T*HE DAY BEFORE Daddy and me were goin' to go to Tennessee to try to find out about my brother, Johnny, I had me one of those summer afternoons that seemed to last forever. I whistled for my dog, Charlie, but he wouldn't come. Too hot for Charlie. I knew he'd be up under the porch, keeping cool. It was so hot the cicadas were chirrin' in the daytime. I didn't pay the heat any mind. I went on down in the woods behind the house to a place I knew where the dirt had washed away, leaving long slabs of rock. Sometimes you'd find a rattlesnake down there soaking up the heat from the rock, but there weren't any around, and I didn't even mind.

I lay on my stomach on the rock and watched a string of black ants struggle through patches of moss and flaky gray lichen. I picked up a twig that had an ant on it and made him walk from one end to the other, swapping hands when he got too near the end. I flipped the stick, and he flew through the air and landed on some dry grass. He seemed kind of fussed up. I reckon the world didn't seem real secure to him any more.

Little gray lizards went from being frozen still with just their throats puffing out to scooting across the hot rock like tiny alligators. I lay real still, and one got up on my hand and walked up my arm. I tried to keep still, but it tickled so much that I had to scare it off and scratch. Then I saw this fat gray squirrel up in a hickory tree. The tree was growing down the hill from me, so the squirrel was about level with me. I groped around for a rock and pulled my slingshot out of my back pocket. I didn't want to hit him, so I aimed for the

tree trunk near the limb he was sitting on. Thwock! I hit it dead center, and that old squirrel jumped like he was on springs and started to cuss.

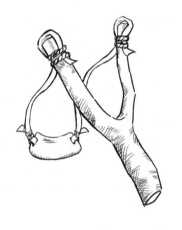

I'd have been having twice as much fun if Butch Jenkins had been over to spend the night, but me and Daddy were goin' to Tennessee the next morning early, so Butch hadn't come over. I thought about climbing our favorite tree where we had started a treehouse, but that wasn't any fun without Butch, so I lay back on the rock and started to think about Johnny.

I was sure that I had seen my twin brother, and that he had seen me. It didn't seem strange to me any more. It was like I'd found a big piece of my life that I hadn't even known was missing. Maybe it was because he was so skinny and dirty, but I was worried about him. What if he was sick? What if we couldn't find him? What if we found him but couldn't help him? All these questions and a bunch more were rattling around in my head, when I realized how hot I was. The breeze had quit, and there I sat on a hot rock in the middle of July in the full sun with the sweat dripping off my nose. I got up and stretched and wiped my face. I needed a drink, so I started on back to the house.

We lived out in the country on Shades Mountain in a one-story, sandstone house, planted all around with box-wood bushes, beds of lilies and azaleas. When I got behind the bushes, I could creep most of the way around the house without being seen. There was ivy growing on the house which made it look older than it was. Daddy's parents, who had died before I was adopted, had built it in 1907. Daddy had kept the house and moved into it in 1925 when he and Momma had gotten married.

There was a big screen porch out front and a little one in the back. During the summer, I got to sleep on one of the daybeds on the front porch, where it was cooler. I'd lay out there and watch the lightning bugs sparking, looking at the stars and listening to the cicadas chirrin' in rhythm. "Chee, chee…chee, chee, chee…chee, chee, chee, chee…cheeeeeee." Then it would start all over again. Sometimes it was real loud, but I was used to those bugs. They put me to sleep. When it rained, Momma would put canvas covers over the daybeds and I'd sleep in my bedroom. There were lots of windows in the house, and it seemed shady and cool inside even during the summer.

Down the hill the drive branched off to a little frame house with a screen porch in front where Jenny May and Jackson Harris lived. Jenny May did the cooking and the laundry for Momma. She had helped to raise me, and would give me a swat on the rear end when I did wrong quicker than Momma would. Next to Momma and Daddy, I loved her the best. Jenny May's husband, Jackson, was a tall, very black colored man, very handsome with a gold tooth in the front of his mouth and deep a bass voice. He could make Jenny May laugh any time he wanted to. Jackson did a little bit of everything; worked in the yard, drove the station wagon, served dinner and sometimes helped Momma with the house cleaning. Beyond the little house was a garage and beyond that was the barn.

Daddy had three Jersey cows and two horses. There was a white man who came in to milk the cows, feed and groom the horses and look after the vegetable garden. His name was Ed Skelton; he talked real funny 'cause he didn't have any teeth and kept a wad of tobacco in his cheek. He was always spitting out tobacco juice, and, seeing as I was always barefoot in the summer, I had to be real careful where I stepped. He was kind of skinny and dried-up looking, so I couldn't tell if he was fifty or seventy. He didn't have much use for me, but once in a while he'd whittle me out a slingshot.

The barn was a good place to hunt rats with a slingshot. There were metal-lined feed bins in the barn, and the feed attracted rats. They were big and ugly and had tunnels all up under the barn. Except for rattlesnakes and moccasins, they were the only thing I would kill. I had shot a robin one time. It made me so sad I knew I wasn't goin' to do any more killing except for dirty, dangerous things that needed killing.

Further on beyond the barn was the vegetable garden where Mr. Skelton tended okra, peas, country gentleman corn, green onions, lettuce, carrots, pole beans and tomatoes. I'd go there and pull up some little carrots and green onions. Water was piped down to the garden from the springhouse, and there was a spigot where I could rinse off the carrots and onions. When you eat things right out of the garden, they taste extra good.

Anyway, I was headed back to the house thinking about getting in the shower. Daddy had built two showers on the back of the house. There was one for ladies and one for men. They were in a little shed-like room open to the outside around the eaves and at the bottom but private. You could hang your clothes on a peg in there and stand on the slats under the shower. On a hot summer day, the cold water that came down from the springhouse felt like heaven. I stood in there and cupped my hands and took a long, cool drink.

After about five minutes in that shower, I felt cool as anything. I climbed into my shorts without drying off, so I would stay cool longer, and went up the steps on the little screen porch and into the kitchen. Jenny May's radio was playing spirituals. Then an announcer was talking about the Smith and Gaston funeral home.

"What's for dinner, Jenny May?"

"Cold fried chicken, honey. I cooked it this morning 'fore it got so hot. Your momma want to have supper on the pavilion this evening. Lord, this here is one hot day. Let's you and me have some lemonade." She got two glasses, and we went out on the back screen porch where the icebox was. I was still thirsty from sweating so much and drank off a big glass while Jenny May was still pouring hers.

"Jenny May, did Momma tell you 'bout Johnny Brasher?"

"Sho did, honey. What you think when you look up and see that boy looking at you?"

"It was mighty funny, Jenny May. I couldn't believe what I was seeing. It was like I was looking at myself. I wish I'd waved, but I was too surprised. I can't stop thinking 'bout him. What if we can't find him?"

"Your Daddy's a smart man, Will. I believe he goin' to find that boy." She got a fried chicken leg out of the icebox and gave it to me.

I had to put on a shirt for supper, but since we were eating out on the pavilion, Momma said I didn't need to put on shoes. The pavilion was separate from the house—a big old porch with a wood shingle roof held up by round posts but no walls. It was a place where you could be indoors and outdoors at the same time. The floor was dark red linoleum, and there were comfortable outdoor chairs with cushions, and a kind of a metal sofa that glided back and forth on a frame, and a porch swing. There were some lamps out there, and a long picnic table where Momma lit candles when supper was set out.

When I came across the stone walk to the pavilion, Daddy had pulled off his jacket and tie and was laying back in a chair with his feet in another one. He was puffing on his pipe, and him and Momma were sipping on tall glasses of ice tea with sprigs of mint sticking up from 'em, which is about the best thing you can drink when it's hot. I got me a glass of ice tea and sat down on the swing. The sun was just goin' down, and there was a pretty sunset over the valley. Momma put her arm around me and gave me a hug. She smelled fresh and sweet like honeysuckle. She was telling Daddy a story.

"So there was cousin Fran, living in that big old house in Nashville with that nice, little colored lady, Luly, looking after

her. Trouble was, Luly was just as old and vague as cousin
Fran. They got groceries sent in and hardly ever went out.
Luly cooked for Fran, and Fran read to Luly in the evenings.
Far as I can tell, they were two happy old souls. Well, anyway,
one afternoon Fran took a notion to go around the garden
which was all grown up and gone to weed, and she wound
up at the back of the house where there was an outdoors en-
trance to the basement. Come to find out there was a whole
family of folks living in the basement. They were white folks
who had lost their farm...man and wife and three little kids.
The man had a job pumping gas but couldn't afford a place to
live. They'd been there for almost a year, and nobody knew it."

"What happened to the folks that were living in the basement?" Daddy asked.

"Stayed right there for two or three years, 'til the man
finally got a better job in a sawmill. The man had already
put up an outhouse which he had hidden back in the bushes.
Cousin Fran had a stove and sink put in for 'em. After that, I
guess she and Luly forgot they were there."

"Lord, Lord," Daddy was shaking his head. "Allie, you do
have some characters in your family. And while we're on the
subject, when Will and I get back from Tennessee, we need
to have your folks to dinner. Let's have Todd and Evelyn and
the kids, too." He was talking about Mama's older brother
and his family. I had grown up with my two cousins, Janie
and Henry Hightower. Janie was a tomboy. She could run
as fast as most boys and would punch you in a second if you
teased her. She was a year older than me. Henry was a year
younger. He was real chubby and an awful tattletale. It was
always fun when the Hightowers came to dinner.

It was evening and it was slowly getting dark. Everything

was looking kind of soft and purple and the fireflies were
out...sparking all around the yard. I couldn't tell whether I
was smelling Mama's perfume or the honeysuckle that grew
on the edge of the woods. Daddy was telling Momma about
some problems he had at the office, and I stopped listening.
My mind went out to the evening star that was hanging
bright and pure out there over the valley, then I saw that
Jackson had gotten the food on the picnic table... beaten biscuits, deviled eggs, potato salad, sliced tomatoes with onions,
and cold fried chicken.

"I'm starving!" I said.

"Let's eat," Daddy said. "Can't have this boy starving on us."

I started with four pieces of chicken.

Chapter Five

Johnny

*I*F THE TRAIN had stopped, I would've got off, but it didn't. We was goin' the wrong way, for sure. I figured I was headed right back to Tennessee, but the train was rolling along too fast to jump. I got tired of waiting for it to stop and climbed back up on the feed sacks.

I must have fell asleep. When I woke up, I could see light shining around the edge of the door. I climbed off the sacks of feed and slid the door open. It was late. The sun was high up in the sky, and it was hot. I sat down inside the car in the shade and watched the fields and woods roll by.

I was some thirsty. I'd been eating ham and crackers, both of which is salty, and I hadn't brung no water. My mouth was so dry, I couldn't have spit for a hundred dollars. I rode along for three or four hours, wondering what it was like to die of thirst, when the train started to slow down. I got up and slid the door almost shut. After a while we slam-banged to a stop, and I peeked out the crack.

I seen a man walking back along the tracks, and I jumped back and scampered up on the sacks of feed to hide. Then I heard something rattle at the end of the car. I heard the train chugging away, but my car wasn't moving. I climbed down off the sacks of feed, slid open the door and looked out. I saw the train disappearing around a bend.

My car was sitting on a siding in the middle of nowhere. There was a stretch of mud that come up almost to the tracks, and, beyond that, mostly water with tall grass and reeds sticking up. It looked like some kind of swamp.

My first idea was to head for that water. I climbed down the bank and slipped and slid across the mud to the edge of the water where my feet went out from under me. I went down hard and found myself settin' next to the biggest water moccasin I'd ever seen. He was draw'd back ready to strike, and I know'd he would soon as I moved. There was a sharp-crack sound, and the snake flipped back, twitching around in the water, and I rolled over and scooted across that mud like a crab.

"Hee! Hee! Hee! Hee! Hee!"

I looked up and there was a little dried-up looking black man sitting in a flat-bottomed boat with his toes hooked over the edge of the seat. He was holding a rifle and laughing like a hyena.

"W-where you come from?" I said.

"Yas, suh, tha's what I gon' ask you, boy. You don' want to go sliding up on no snakes like that. Hee! Hee! I never see no white boy look whiter that you did settin' down with that snake. Hee, hee, hee! Oh, Law!" He stepped out of the boat while he was still laughing, onto the same mud that had

threw me, and, sure enough, his feet scooted out, and down he went on his rear end. I started to laugh, too, as he got up...real careful. He was scowling at me.

"Don't you know 'nuff not to be laughing at yo' elders?" he said. I tried to quit laughing and mostly got it stopped. Then he started to grin and turned away, trying to hide it. "'Less the elder be the kind of old fool that fall on his butt in the mud! Then I guess a boy's 'titled to some laughing. Hee! Hee! Ain't you and me a couple of fools slippin' 'round in this here mud? Hee! Hee!"

"I want to thank you for shooting that snake," I said. "Why, sho . . . I don't normally shoot no snakes. Live and let live I says; but that'un fixin' to whomp you."

"I come off that boxcar," I said. "I was climbing down the bank to get a drink. Is this here Tennessee or Alabama?"

"Law, chile, you in Georgia...'bout a hunnert mile from Savannah. You a long way from Alabama and Tennessee. This here the Blackwater Swamp, and don't you never go drinking no swamp water. You poop yo'self inside out."

"I got to have me a drink," I said. "I been eating ham and soda crackers since yesterday, and I ain't had no water."

"Well, come on then. I got me a jug of rainwater in the skiff."

I walked real careful over to the little creek where the boat was tied up to a stump. Then I saw that the grass flats was full of these wandery channels twisting this way and that. He reached into the boat and handed me a glass jug half full of water. I near 'bout drunk it dry.

"Whew!" I said. "That's a heap better. Good thing for me you come along. How come you did come along? What you called?"

"Name's Abraham Lincoln Fraiser. Don't see many folks, but, when I does, they calls me Linc. I come here to borrow some of that pig food off the boxcar. My dog purely love that pig food. They's a road that go East over on the other side of the tracks. Big old pig farm up that way owned by some folks name of Scagg. They gets a car-load of feed dropped here by the train to Savannah, and here it sets 'til they comes down and picks it up wif a truck. Sometime that feed set here fo' a week 'fo they picks it up. I usually borrows a sack or two for my dog to eat on.

"Them Scaggs has caused me some grief from time to time, so I believes I has it comin'. Boy, that freight train don't come out of Savannah but twice a week, so you ain't gon' nowhere fo' a while. What you called?"

"I'm Johnny. My last name is 'sposed to be Brasher, but I wish it weren't. My folks was killed when I was real little. My aunt took me in. She's a Brasher, but I don't belong to her. I'm running away."

"What you mean, you don't belong to her, chile? Yo' aunt done tuk you in, didn't she?"

"Yeah, but she don't care nothing 'bout me. She was always sending me to bed without nothing to eat and whippin' on my legs. Didn't hardly talk to me. Sarah heard her say she didn't care nothing 'bout me. I don't want to be no Brasher." Linc looked at my legs.

"My, my! Folks can be some mean. Who Sarah?"

"Sarah worked for my aunt. She took care of me. Used to try to get me off whippings and sneak me food when I wasn't 'sposed to have none. Aunt Min treated her 'bout as bad as she treated me. The only reason Sarah stayed with Aunt Min was on account of wanting to help me. I couldn't have stood being there without Sarah. I told Sarah if she got fired, I was goin' to run off. Sure enough, Aunt Min fired her, and I run off. Got on that freight train. It was heading towards Birmingham. I reckon my car got dropped off and picked up by another train."

Linc was studying me.

"What you gon' do now?" he asked.

"I guess I got to walk up that road and find me that pig farm," I told him.

"Boy, that pig farm twenty mile off. If you was to get there, them Scaggs ain't good folks. Ain't never seen the women, but them menfolks is mean…white trash. I tries not to see 'em. Talks to me like I was dirt. Call me 'nigger.' No count folks. Always drunk and wanting to fight." He sat there studying me. "You was trying to get to Birmingham on that train? How come Birmingham?"

"I think I got a brother there. I want to find him." "What you mean, 'brother'?" Linc asked, so I had to tell him about Will. We climbed in the skiff and sat there, and I started in on the story.…

". . . so he was on the Birmingham passenger train and, according to Sarah, his name's Will and he was took in by some folks name Jennison. I reckon if I can get to Birmingham, I might can find him."

"Well if that don't beat all!" Linc said. "Hee! Hee! You settin' by the tracks and yo' twin brother come by on the train. You say he look a lot like you?"

"He wasn't like me. He was me, only cleaner and nicer. He seen me, too. I seen his eyes get big."

Linc sat there thinking.

"Boy, what I gon' do wif you? My, my...." He thought some more. "Look here, chile,...there ain't nothing else to do. You got to come wif me. You and me gone be stuck wif each other fo' a while. I cain't leave you here, so you jes' got to come wif me. That freight out of Savannah that go up to the L&N tracks to Birmingham don't come back through here 'til next week, so you stuck. You got to come wif me."

He climbed out of the skiff.

"First thing we got to do is get my pig food. Hooter gon' be one sorry dog, if I don' bring back a sack of that pig food." We walked, slipping and sliding across the mud flat to the tracks. I climbed up in the boxcar and drug a sack of feed over to the door. He put it on his shoulder, and we went on back and put the feed in the middle of the boat. I climbed in and sat in the front. Link stood in the back and picked up the pole. Then he pushed us out into the creek with a long, smooth stroke and twisted the pole loose from the mud.

"Where we goin', Linc?"

"We gon' in the swamp, Johnny. Linc live up in Blackwater Swamp...way on up in that swamp."

Chapter Six

Will

WE GOT UP TO Columbia about one in the afternoon. It was hot. What else, July in Tennessee. Daddy had telegraphed Mr. Simmons, the L&N Station Master in Columbia, to try to get us a list of Brashers who lived north of town. When the train got in, Mr. Simmons was waiting for us with the list in his hand. We went into his office in the station house and he told Daddy about the Brashers he had located.

"There aren't but five Brasher families up near that water stop, Mr. Frank. The sheriff ought to be able to tell you more about them. His office is right in the courthouse on the square. Name's Dave Pratt. Good man. Tell him who you are. He'll do anything he can for you."

"I sure thank you, Leighton," Daddy said. "Were you able to get us a room in the hotel?"

"Yes, sir, that was easy. Not many folks staying in the Bethel this time of year. I'm durned if I know how they keep the place open. Do you need the company car while you're here?"

"That would be mighty helpful, Leighton. How you goin' to get home if we take the car?"

"No problem there, Mr. Jennison. I just live four blocks over from the station."

⌒⌒⌒

Sheriff Pratt was a small man with lanky brown hair combed over a bald spot and deep-cut wrinkles around his eyes, which were pale blue. His face was sunburned except for his forehead which was fish-belly white. He wore a black suit with a badge on his coat. Daddy introduced himself and me and sat down and told him the story.

"All we want to do is see the boy, Sheriff, and make sure he's all right. Would you have any idea if any of the Brashers on this list have a redheaded boy?"

"Mr. Jennison, I think I know who you're looking for. Most of them Brashers north of town are pretty rough. Two or three of 'em make moonshine whiskey. They used to run me crazy. I finally just give up on trying to catch 'em. Most of them rough Brashers have lots of kids. Wouldn't adopt nobody; but there's a preacher up there name of Joe Brasher. Married an old maid. Seems to me I heard some time ago about him and his wife taking in a kid. I can show you on the map just about where their place is."

Sheriff Pratt walked over to a big map he had on the wall. "Right about here," he said, putting an X on the map. "Just past where this dirt road crosses this little creek." We walked over to look at the big map on the sheriff's wall.

"Will, I bet you that's the place. It's not half a mile from the tank where the train stops to take on water." Daddy shook hands with the sheriff and thanked him.

We pulled up to the Brasher place. It didn't look like much. There was an old frame house with a sagging front porch. The paint was peeling off. The yard was all weedy and there were a couple of tumbled down sheds and a sorry looking barn.

We went up to the front door and knocked. My heart was hammering. This skinny, angry-looking woman came to the door. I could see a man standing behind her in the shadows. Before she could say anything, she saw me. She went pale and stepped back, and her eyes went wide.

"Miz Brasher, my name's Frank Jennison." Daddy put his hand on my shoulder, "this is my adopted son, Will. I believe there is a possibility that you adopted a boy called Johnny who is Will's natural twin brother. We'd like to see him, if we could."

"He ain't here no more," the woman said. "He's gone. Run away. Good riddance to him." She kind of spit out the words.

"Run away?" said Daddy. "When?"

"Must have run off last Friday, the same day we left. Worthless, ungrateful boy. We took him in. Give him a good home. First time we leave him alone he runs off."

"First time you left him alone?" Daddy asked.

"We had a three-day revival meetin' to go to. He was supposed to take care of the critters while we was gone. All he did was turn the pig loose and run off. I hope he don't come back."

"Let me get this straight, madam," Daddy says, his eyes starting to glint. "You left the boy alone for three days. Now he's been missing for nearly a week. Have you reported that to the sheriff?"

She stuck her pointed face out and narrowed her eyes at Daddy.

"What business is that of yours, Mister?" She kind of hissed like a snake. "It's none of your damn business. Fancy dressin', stuck up city man, think you can walk in my house accusin' me! God will curse folks like you. Just who do you think you are? Get off my place, damn you!" By this time, she was shrieking and actually starting to froth. White spit was at the corners of her mouth and her eyes were bugging out. Daddy's eyes were frosty now. He drew himself up and raised one eyebrow.

"Goodbye, madam," he said. He spun around and pushed me ahead of him. She was standing in the door still shrieking and cursing.

"You belong in Hell with that Johnny. God will punish you . . ."

We walked away as fast as we could, but we could still hear her ranting and screeching behind us.

"What a horror!" Daddy muttered to himself. "No wonder the boy ran away." Mr. Brasher must have come out the back door and walked down to the barn near where we had parked the car. He spoke to Daddy without looking at either of us.

"You want to find that boy, Mister, you ought to talk to the colored lady who used to cook for us. Name's Sarah Davis. Works for Miz Barncastle. The place is on Munger Street back in towards town. Sarah's the one took care of Johnny. She might know something 'bout where he's at."

"Thank you, sir, that's very kind of you," Daddy answered.

"I'm sorry my wife went at you like that," the man said. "She ain't quite right in the head."

"Indeed, sir," Daddy said.

It wasn't hard to find the right place. We found Munger Street, and Daddy asked an old colored man who was working in a yard if he knew the Barncastle house.

"Yas'm, hit's right over yonder," he said pointing to a pretty, old brick house that was two doors down and across the street.

We left the car where it was and walked over to the house. I rang the bell, and a nice-looking colored lady answered the door.

"Yes, suh?" she said, then she saw me. "My land!" she said. "You mus' be Johnny's brother."

"I am," I said. "I'm Will. Are you Sarah?"

"I am, honey. I look after yo' brother bes' I could since he was two years old. You Mister Jennison, suh?"

"That's right," said Daddy shaking hands with Sarah. "How'd you know our names?"

"Heard Miz Brasher talkin' about you folks. Miz Barncastle's right poorly today. She got a weak heart, and the doctor say she got to stay in bed. If youall come on through to the kitchen, suh, I can give you something cool to drink."

"Thank you, Sarah," Daddy said.

We followed Sarah into the kitchen and sat at the kitchen table while she fixed us some ice tea.

Daddy said, "Sarah, we've just been out to the Brasher place. Mrs. Brasher didn't take kindly to my asking questions. She was very bitter towards the boy. I suppose she didn't treat him very well…am I right?"

"Yes, suh, you sho is. That's one mean woman. I swear, I believe she would've starve Johnny, if I hadn't been sneaking him food. You should've seen the back of his legs. All stripe up from her whipping him. He never done nothing bad. Not nothing to deserve that kind of punishment. He's a sweet boy. Something the matter with that woman." "You're right about that, Sarah. I believe the woman is insane. It's a wonder you could stand to work for her." "I stayed on to be there with Johnny," she said. "Thank God you did," Daddy told her.

"When Miz Brasher fire me, Johnny, he say he gon' to run away. I know'd he was too young to be on his own, but seem to me anything was better than him being alone with that woman. I give him five dollars and told him to be careful who he took up with."

"Sarah, do you have any idea where he went?" Daddy asked her.

"Yes, suh, I do. That chile all the time gon' down to watch the trains go by. Tha's how he come to see his brother." She looked down at me. "When he say he seen a boy on the Birmingham train that looked just like him, I went ahead and told him what I heard Mister and Miz Brasher saying that time. Tol' him his aunt and uncle say he was a twin and that he prob'ly had a brother name Will who had been took in by somebody name Jennison. When I ask him where he was goin' to run off to, he say, 'Birmingham.' I reckon he climb on one of those freight trains goin' to Birmingham, Mr. Jennison. I sho do."

Daddy took some money out of his billfold.

"Sarah, I want to give you back the money you gave the boy, and the rest of this is a gift from our family to show our appreciation for the way you took care of Johnny even when you wanted to leave."

"Thank you, suh. I loves that boy, Mr. Jennison."

"I know you do, Sarah, and you'll never know how much we appreciate that."

That evening we had dinner in the Bethel Hotel. We had been back to see the sheriff and reported Johnny missing. The sheriff said he would put out the word, but that we ought to talk to the police in Birmingham. He thought Johnny might turn up there. We went back to the L&N Station, and Mr. Simmons helped us get Johnny's description out to all the stations between there and Birmingham; then Daddy called the Birmingham police. He knew the chief personally and was able to get him on the phone and tell him the story.

Then he called Momma and told her what we had found out. He told her he had to talk some business with Mr. Simmons in the morning, and that we would catch the afternoon train to Birmingham. He asked her to have Jackson meet the train.

Daddy said that pretty soon there would be a whole lot of folks looking for Johnny. Still, later on, when we were having dinner, I could tell he was worried. We sat in the big dining room of the old hotel under a slow ceiling fan. Counting us, there weren't ten people in the whole place. The waiter brought us country-fried steak, green beans and rice and gravy. There were corn muffins, too, but neither one of us could eat very much.

We finished dinner and went out on the porch and sat in two big rocking chairs. Daddy lit his pipe. The little town had gone quiet. There were a couple of dusty-looking cars parked on Garden Street. The street lights showed how empty the street was. It was a hot, dark night and we sat there rocking and looking at the lonely little town.

"Trouble is, son, riding on a freight train is a tricky thing. It's dangerous to begin with, but not only that, freight trains get busted up as they go along. Cars get split out and picked up by other trains. Someone who doesn't know what they're doing can wind up where they don't want to be."

"How are we ever goin' to find him?" I asked.

"Well, son, there's not much more we can do now. We've just got to wait and hope he turns up."

"Yes, sir," I said. "I don't know why, but I think he's all right."

"Sometimes twins have a feeling for each other, Will, even at a distance. Your hunch may have something to it. We've got something else goin' for us...he's your twin, so he's bound to be smart. I think he'll look after himself better than most kids would." He put his hand over mine when he said that and it made me feel good.

Later that night, we were in bed and Daddy had turned off the light. The room was hot, and I lay on the sheets with nothing over me, feeling sweat where my head and neck were on the pillow.

"It's like it's me wandering around out there somewhere," I said to Daddy.

"Will, I can promise you one thing," he said. "When we find your brother—and I think we will find him eventually—I'm goin' to move heaven and earth to get him into our family. He's never goin' back to that awful woman; not if I can help it."

The way he said this was so quiet and strong that it made me feel like everything was goin' to work out. I heaved a big sigh.

"Daddy?"

"What, son?"

"I'm so glad you and Momma want Johnny." "We sure do want him, Will."

"Night, Daddy," I said. He reached over and squeezed my shoulder.

"Night, son."

Chapter Seven

Johnny

LINC POLED THE BOAT through the twisty little channels in the grass and mud flats 'til we come to a deep, narrow creek; then, he put down the pole and slid some oars out from under the board seats. He started to row. It was amazing how fast he could make that skiff move.

"This here crick hook up to Blackwater River," he said. "The river go on up through the swamp where Linc's place is. Hard to find my place if you don't know where it is. Not many folks can find it, and that suit Linc jes' fine."

"Why don't you want to be found, Linc?"

"Well, boy, like I tol' you, they some mean folks live roun' an' 'bout this here swamp. Linc don't mess with them, and they don't mess with Linc. Can't bother somebody if you can't find 'em. Hee, hee! Some folks call Linc the swamp ghost."

The creek come into a bigger river and we dropped down with the current.

"This here the easy part," said Linc. "River do all the work."

I seen why it was called the Blackwater River. The water was so dark brown it was almost black. Linc rowed to the far shore and pulled up to a cypress knee that was sticking out of the water. He reached into the water.

"Got me a trotline out here, Johnny. We be lucky, be a catfish on it." He pulled the line in hand over hand. "Sho 'nuff, somethin' on this here line." He got to the second-to-last hook and flipped a big catfish into the bottom of the boat. "Good eatin' tonight, Johnny. Catfish stew! Yas, suh!"

The fish flopped around in the bottom of the skiff 'til Linc pulled out a belt knife and cut off its head, which he took to bait up the trotline again. The boat spun around in a circle while Linc got the oars. There was dark-looking swamp on the left. Cyprus trees. Spanish moss hanging down. Linc rowed into a creek, and the trees closed in over us.

After about five minutes rowing through the gloom, we followed a branch to the right. It seemed to wind around like a snake. The creek forked twice more, and we went right and then left. I was already lost. I couldn't have got out of that swamp if my life depended on it. Finally, Linc pulled over to some branches and vines that were hanging down and said, "Duck down." I done what he said. And we slid under the branches into another creek that went off to the left.

Up ahead, I could see some high ground like an island in the swamp. The creek split again and straddled the island. We glided along the back side of the island where the creek widened out. The view opened up to more grass and mud flats as far as you could see. Linc pulled the skiff up to a small, weather-beaten dock. There on the dock was the ugliest dog I ever did see.

"Tha's Hooter," Linc said. "Somebody's bloodhound took up with a mastiff an' out come Hooter. Ain't she ugly? Hee,

hee! Ugliest dog in the world. She don't take to folks, but you leave her alone she won't bother you."

Hooter was laying with her head between her paws, wagging her tail and curling her lips up off her front teeth, grinning like a idiot. She was huge with big mournful eyes, tattered-up ears and a scarred head about the size of a small watermelon. She was gray and brown, and her big tail thumped the dock like a two-by-four.

I climbed out on the dock, and before I could stand up, Hooter come over and give me a good sniffing.

"Hey, Hooter," I says, and Hooter commenced lickin' my face and then rolled over on her back to have her belly rubbed. I obliged, and Hooter moaned with pleasure.

"Well, I be dang!" Linc said. "Hooter, you a hussy! You makin' a liar out of Linc. Hee, hee, hee! She ain't never tuk to nobody before."

"I love dogs," I says.

We unloaded the skiff and Linc put the catfish on a little

table that was nailed on the dock. In 'bout a minute he had the fish skinned and gutted.

"Look here, Johnny," he says as he threw the guts and skin off the dock. "Come see Hepburn." There was a swirl in the water about twenty feet off the dock, and a big gator slid up and took the fish scraps.

"That a alligator, Linc?" I says, stepping back from the edge of the dock.

"Sho is, boy. He the garbage man. Eat jus' about any- thing, even if it ain't no good to eat."

"He's huge, Linc. He mus' be ten feet long."

"Mo'. Mo' like thirteen, fourteen foot. I calls him Hepburn after one of my cousins who was big and mean. You know, Johnny, all mean folks ain't white. They some mean colored folks, too. That cousin of mine used to scare me to death. He carry a razor and had the evilest eye I ever see. He cut up two folks purty bad and got sent off to prison. Now this old gator here, I ain't too scared of him. He so spoilt from eatin' my fish scraps he prob'ly forgot how to catch his own food. Still, don't you be doin' no swimmin' off this here dock. The garbage man lazy, but I don't trust no gator.

"You wants to get in the water…over the other side of the island they's a little beach. Nice place to swim."

"I wouldn't swim off this dock for a hunnert dollars," I said.

Hooter was sniffing around the pig feed, and Linc picked it up and walked across some planks to the island. Sitting up there in the cypress trees was the dangdest little house I ever seen. It was so gray and weathered it looked like it grew there. The bottom of the house was nailed onto the stumps of cypress trees that had been cut off two-foot-tall so the house was up off the ground. The house was kind of round, and one big cypress grew right up through the middle of it. The rafters had been nailed right onto this tree, and it held up the center of the roof. The roof was made out of sheets of tin. The front part of the roof sloped down to a kind of gutter made out of boards that tilted down to carry rainwater to a downspout that went into a barrel on the porch. The sides of the house was made out of weathered gray boards nailed on up-and-down, with strips of wood covering the cracks.

The whole thing kind of hunkered down on the island. There was a live oak tree shading the porch, and Spanish moss hanging down all around.

"Come on in, Johnny. Make yo'self at home."

Link carried the sack of feed into the house and I followed him. He slit the burlap bag with his pocketknife and poured the feed into a barrel. He got an old tin plate and scooped up some of the feed and took it out to Hooter. Then Linc came back in and hung up his rifle on a couple of pegs over the door. There was a shotgun hung up just over the rifle.

Inside, the house was all one room with the tree coming up the middle of it. There was a old kitchen table and a couple of kitchen chairs. There was iron hooks nailed in the tree with cooking stuff, pots and what all, hanging on 'em. There was hooks in the rafters with three hams and some burlap bags of stuff hanging down from 'em. One side of the room was the kitchen with a counter and some shelves and a little stove made out of a metal barrel. There was a stove pipe that run out through the roof. The other side of the room had a bunk built onto the wall and some more shelves for clothes and stuff.

Linc stuck some dry moss and sticks in the stove and popped a kitchen match with his thumb nail and started a fire. When the fire was goin' good, he put a pot of water on the stove, cut up the catfish into chunks and put 'em in the pot. He opened a tin box and took out a chunk of salt pork and cut off some slices. Then he put a flat iron pan that looked like a griddle on the stove next to the pot.

"This here side meat so full of salt it don't hardly go bad." He threw the pork on the griddle. "We got to fix you up a place to sleep, Johnny." He reached under a bunk that was built onto the wall and pulled out some folded up quilts. "This here gon' make a fine bed." He piled the folded quilts on top of each other. "That gon' feel mighty good after ridin' in a boxcar.

"Come on, boy, let's get us some wild onions." We went out a door on the other side of the house and down a few steps onto the island. We walked up a path through the cypress and oak trees, and Linc pointed up another little path.

"Outhouse up there, Johnny," Linc said.

We went about fifty yards to the other side of the island, where there was a grassy stretch and a small beach. Hooter followed us and walked down to the beach where she lay down in the water. A big gray bird with a long bill was wading on the far side of the creek looking for fish. Linc said it was a heron. Near the edge of the grass was a patch of wild onions. Linc pulled out a handful and walked over to the water to rinse 'em off. I went with him and washed the mud off of my hands and arms.

"If you wants to swim, Johnny, this here the bes' spot," Linc said. "Just stay near the beach and keep yo' eyes open fo' gators and snakes. Ain't never seen no gators on this side, but it don't hurt to look."

When we got back, I asked him about the house. "Did you make this place, Linc?"

"Sho. A man I works for sometimes, Mr. Franklin Webb,

had a lots of ol' lumber. Tol' me I could have all I wanted
and let me use his plantation work boat to haul it over here.
Give me some copper screenin' too, an tha's a good thing.
If I didn't have no screen on my windows, I'd be ate up by
skeeters come sundown. After I made 'bout ten trips in that
work boat, I had me enough stuff to build this here house.

"Mr. Webb a fine man. I still help him out some. Keep an
eye on the Webb plantation house when he ain't there, and
I takes him fishin' when he is. I makes 'nuff money to buy
what I needs to keep gon' out here: Corn meal, black-eyed
peas, ham, coffee, ammunition...few other little things.

"Mr. Webb, he come to the plantation in the winter-time.
Res' the time, that old house stan' empty. It's a great big
ol' house. Full of ol' furniture...silver...I don't know what
all. My daddy was a slave on the Webb plantation. When
the Yankees come through durin' the war, General Sherman
done burnt mos' the plantation houses, but the Webb house
far 'nuff out here in the swamp so the Yankees didn't find
it. The Webbs was nice folks. Daddy be free by then, but he
like the Webbs and he stay on.

"Durin' the war and after it, come to that, there wasn't
'nuff food. Daddy hunt and fish in the swamp...help to feed
the Webb family and the colored folks that stay on wif 'em.
When Colonel Webb git back from the war and foun' out
what Daddy had done, he give Daddy a nice little house wif
a piece of land. The Colonel and Daddy come to be mighty
close friends. Well, Daddy live in that little house wif me
and Momma, but what he love was this here swamp. Used
to say the swamp was where he really feel free.

"When I was 'bout yo' age, Daddy start bringin' me in
the swamp. Taught me how to hunt an' fish...find my way

around in the swamp. My daddy was right. A man free in the swamp. That's why Linc build up this here little house."

We went on back to the house, and Linc chopped up the wild onions and threw 'em in the pot along with a pinch of black pepper. He got him a handful of rice out of a can and threw that in the pot. Then he chopped up the crispy pieces of salt pork and threw that in, too.

"This here stew got to simmer some," Linc said, lighting his pipe. He stretched out on his bunk. "Le's you and me res' up while it's cookin', Johnny. Linc done a lots a rowin' today."

I stretched out on the quilts and lay there thinking…listening to Linc puffing on his pipe. I must've dozed off. When Hooter come up and put her cold nose on my face, it woke me up quick. I sat up and hollered: "What!" When I seen Hooter, I remembered where I was. Then I smelled that stew. I hadn't ate nothing but ham and crackers and cheese since I run off, and that stew smelled some good. Linc stretched and got up and went outside to knock out his pipe. When he come back in he went over to the counter and started to mix up a corn-meal batter in a can.

"You hungry, Johnny?" Linc asked.

"Linc, I could eat the back end off a skunk," I told him. "My, my!" Linc chuckled. "This here stew gon' be mo' better than that. Be ready in jes' a minute." He picked up the can of cornmeal batter and poured three or four dabs of it into the pork fat on the griddle. They popped and frizzled and smoked. When the edges turned brown, he flipped them over. Soon he was stacking up crispy, thin corn cakes an' I was swallowing every two or three seconds.

Me and Hooter went out on the porch. The sun was goin' down, and the whole sky over the flats had gon' red and gold all mixed in with streaks of dark blue. Hooter come up and put her nose in my hand. I kneeled down and give her a hug. Linc come out and leaned on the railing.

"Look at that, Linc."

"Ain't it a glory!" said Linc.

All of a sudden, it was almost dark. As I looked out over the creek I saw what looked like two hot coals glowing in the black water.

"What's that, Linc?" I said pointing.

"Tha's the garbage man," Linc told me. "Gator eyes glows like that."

"Scary lookin'!" I said. "Sho is, Johnny."

The bugs was getting bad, so we ducked inside. Hooter, too, but she had good manners and didn't mooch no food. Linc lit a kerosene lantern and hung it from the rafter over the table, then he dished up the stew. I like to died, it tasted so good. I ate and ate, taking bites of the crispy, greasy corn cakes and mixing them in with bites of the stew.

"I ain't never had nothin' this good," I told Linc.

"Bein' hungry always make the cook look good," said Linc, who was eating his share. "Sho am glad that was a big catfish. Be enough left fo' breakfast."

"Catfish stew for breakfast?" I asked him.

"We ain't got no icebox, Johnny. Got to eat up stuff fo' it spoil."

Linc had a can of Prince Albert tobacco on the table and he packed a corn cob pipe and fired it up. He tipped his chair back against the counter and sat there with his feet on the rungs looking at me and puffing on his pipe.

"You ever play checkers, Johnny?"

"I'm pretty good at checkers, Linc. Sarah taught me. I

could beat her sometimes." I was leaning on the table holding my head up with both hands.

"Tomorrow night, we gon' play some checkers, but, right now, you got to get some sleep. You can pee off the dock, but make sho you don't pee in the boat. There's some moon tonight, so you can see what you doin'."

I went down to the dock, but I didn't stand too close to the edge. I was thinking about them hot-coal eyes out in that black water. When I come back, I stopped at the water barrel on the porch. I took up the dipper and had a long, cool drink. When I went in, Linc was still sitting at the table smoking his pipe and humming some old song. I stumbled over to the quilts and flopped down. It was like my bones kind of melted into that pile of quilts. I was feeling full and happy.

I was way out in the middle of a swamp, but with Linc settin' there puffing his pipe and humming under his breath, I felt safe and peaceful. I heaved a big, jaw-breaker yawn.

"Night, Linc," I said "Night, Johnny." "Linc?"

"Here I is," he said.

"I sure appreciate you lettin' me stay with you."

"Sho, Johnny. Linc don't get many folks to visit. I be glad to have you."

Bugs was singing and a bullfrog was chunkin'. Linc's pipe smelled good. I heard some bird calling up in the swamp . . .

Chapter Eight

Will

I'D BEEN HAVING my
dream but it was differ-
ent now. It was the picnic
dream again. We were walking away from the quilt, but
when I looked up at Momma,
she had red hair.

"Come on, Johnny," she
said, and I looked back at
the quilt but Johnny wasn't
there. "Where is he?" Momma said and started to call

him. "He's all right, Momma," I said. "Don't worry." Then I
woke up in the daybed on the screen porch.

It was early. I heard a rooster crow from down in the
chicken yard. The early morning air smelled good. It smelled
like things were goin' to happen. I remembered Butch was
coming over to spend the night. I stretched and lay there
thinking about Johnny.

The day after we got back from Tennessee, Daddy took me downtown and had my picture made. Then he had some reward posters printed up and got 'em sent around by the police and the railroad, but we still hadn't heard anything. Daddy said there was no way of knowing if Johnny had gotten on a freight train or which one or where he had ended up. He was just gone. I thought about him every day, but I wasn't worried. I still felt like he was all right. Daddy came out on the screen porch.

"Morning, Will. Want to go for a ride?" "Yes, sir! Sure do. Morning, Daddy." "Meet you down at the barn, son."

Daddy threw a saddle on Prince, his big gelding and worked the bit into his mouth, then we saddled up Jasmine, the little mare. She danced away when I mounted, but I was used to her ways and swung into the saddle. Daddy had an English saddle, but mine was Western. Jasmine could be a little jumpy sometimes, but with the saddle horn to hang on to, I never fell off.

Soon we were trotting down the drive to the dirt road where we could pick up the bridle path. The sun was just coming up over the trees, and the air still smelled fresh and cool. We were in the woods following the trail on the side of the mountain. At a wide place in the trail, Daddy reigned in Prince to let Jasmine come alongside.

"Butch coming over today, son?" Daddy asked me. "Yes, sir, he's goin' to spend the night."

"What are you boys going to do?"

"Don't know. Might shoot at some rats. Go exploring in

the woods. Me and Butch always got something to do."

"That Butch is a nice boy."

"He is, Daddy. I guess he's my best friend."

"You boys do have a way of getting into trouble some-times. Still, I guess that's part of being a boy."

"Yes, sir," I said, changing some plans I had for me and Butch.

We rode nearly down to Mountain Brook then Daddy pulled up, and we started back. By the time we got back to the barn and unsaddled the horses, we were mighty hungry. We walked up to the house, and, sure enough, Jenny May had breakfast under way. There's nothing like an early morning ride to give you an appetite.

There were sliced peaches on the table, and I scooped some into a bowl. There was a pitcher of heavy cream. It was too thick to pour. I had to get a spoon and help it out of the pitcher. When I sprinkled sugar on those peaches and heavy cream, I had me something mighty good. Daddy did the same as me, and we just sat there eating and smiling at each other. Then Jenny May brought in a dish of grits and a platter of crisp bacon and poached eggs.

"Morning, Jenny May," Daddy said.

"Morning, Mister Frank. You think six eggs goin' to be enough for you and Mister Will?"

"Plenty, Jenny May. Looks wonderful, as usual." She went back in the kitchen and reappeared with a plate stacked-up with toast. We started to help ourselves.

I loved to watch Daddy eat. He'd cut a piece of toast, spear it with his fork in his left hand and spread some country butter on it. Then, using his knife, he'd pile bacon, poached egg and grits in the back of his fork and pop the whole bite in his mouth. I learned his way of doing this, and there isn't any better way to eat breakfast.

Momma always had toast and bacon and coffee on a tray in bed. She said if she ate a breakfast like we had, she'd never keep her figure. She believed in walking; and every morning, when the weather was nice, she'd walk a mile and a half down our dirt road to the highway and back. She was really moving out when she walked. She was beautiful and young-looking. Daddy said she looked more like twenty five than thirty five. Momma loved to read and work in her flower garden. She did a lot of the housework herself.

After Daddy had left for the office, and Momma had gone on her walk, I was hanging around waiting for Jackson to get back with Butch. Jackson had taken the station wagon into Mountain Brook to the Hills store to get some groceries Jenny May needed. After he had been to the store, he was goin' to pick up Butch.

I wandered on back to the kitchen and asked Jenny May if she would make a couple of sandwiches for me and Butch to take in the woods. She said she would when she had time, but she was busy washing up the vegetables Mr. Skelton had brought from the garden, and she chased me out of the kitchen. I went back to my room and got my slingshot and ambled on down to the garage to the tool room where there was a bucket of rusty nuts and bolts. I was goin' to get a handful of steel nuts to use for ammunition shooting at rats.

There were a couple of old bicycle inner tubes hanging on the wall, and I got one down and stood in it to see how far I could stretch it with my arms. The rubber was still good, and it stretched as far as I could reach, and I got to wondering something. I had an inspiration…a flash of genius. Maybe all great ideas come like that. By the time Butch showed up, I was hard at work on the world's biggest slingshot.

I cut one of the inner tubes and clipped out the valve so I had a seven foot long piece of rubber. I looped one end of the tube through a hole I had cut in a foot-long piece of chamois and tied the loop closed with waxed twine. Then I cut the other inner tube and tied it on the same way to the other side of the chamois. Jackson must have gotten back 'cause I heard Butch whistling for me.

We both knew how to whistle with our fingers in our mouths, and I didn't have any trouble hearing him. I stuck my fingers in my mouth and gave him a blast to let him know where I was, and he came running to the garage. Butch was blond with freckles. He was shorter than me and skinny, but he was wiry and quick. When we wrestled, sometimes I beat him and sometimes he beat me.

"Hey, Willie," Butch said. "What you doin' down here?"

"Makin' something, Butch." I showed him what I had.

"What do you think this is?"

"Slingshot," said Butch, who was smarter than most folks. I felt kind of deflated.

"Well, heck, how'd you know?"

"Had to be. What we goin' to shoot at?"

"Listen here, Butch. I got a plan. We'll hike that trail down to Mountain Brook. You know that place on the side of the mountain where you can look down at the Hankley house?" Butch nodded.

"Well, here's what we're goin' to do…"

'Long about noontime, we got down to a kind of ridge where we could see the Hankley place. We sat down and ate our sandwiches and drank a couple of Co'Colas that had gotten warm. The Hankley place was a good two hundred feet lower down than we were and quite a ways off. There was a big, smooth lawn around the house, and I could see a colored man working in the flower beds. He looked about a inch tall.

"Gosh, Willie, you think we can shoot that far?" Butch said.

"Let's give her a try," I said, and we started to tie one side of the inner tube to a tree on the edge of the ridge. We tied the other piece of tube to another tree about six feet away from the first. I dumped about a dozen green tomatoes out of my pack and picked one out for the first shot. I folded that tomato into the piece of chamois, took a good grip and started to walk backwards until the inner tubes were stretched maybe ten feet long; then I turned loose. That green tomato took off like a bullet. We could see it sailing towards the house, but it fell short and landed in the woods on the edge of the Hankley yard. I saw the colored man stand up and look around to see what had made the sound.

"Hot Dog!" said Butch. "We got to give her a little more power!"

For the second shot, I backed up about twelve feet. Butch had to help. He grabbed me around the waist to keep me from sliding. We stretched about as far as we could, and I let go. That shot made it to the yard. The tomato hit the grass and rolled maybe fifty feet. It rolled right past the Hankley yard man. When he saw that tomato rolling across the yard, he jumped up and looked around for sure, scratching his head. He picked up the tomato and walked over to the edge of the woods, but the woods were thin, and he could see there wasn't anybody there. Butch fell to the ground laughing, and I went down on my knees.

"Oh, oh, oh, Lord!" he gasped. "Oh, he can't tell, he can't figure…Oh…Lord! What a mystery."

"Yeah!" I gasped, trying to get my breath. "Green tomatoes from heaven! This is wonderful! Let's give him another shot."

This time we loaded up two tomatoes, but the yard man had gone up to the door. Mrs. Hankley came out, and the colored man showed her the tomato. They both walked out in the yard, so we pulled back and let fly with the third shot. Those two green tomatoes came rolling up to Mrs. Hankley just like she called a couple of dogs. Talk about confused. She and that yard man were walking around in circles, looking all around and waving their arms. You got to know when to quit…not that we were that smart. We just couldn't get up off the ground for laughing. We couldn't have fired off another shot for a hundred dollars. My stomach hurt. When I finally got my wind back, and looked over the edge of the ridge, there was nobody in the yard. It was just as well, 'cause they might have figured it out if we had kept on shooting.

~ ~ ~

That evening me and Butch and Momma were on the pavilion waiting on Daddy to get home from the office. Momma had just pulled a tick off me from behind my ear. Butch was reading a comic book, Momma had a sure-enough book, and I was down on the floor tickling Charlie's paw with a broom straw. His hind foot was kicking like a mule. You'd think a dog would just get up and walk off, but they don't.

Daddy came out on the pavilion, pulling off his tie. He had the newspaper.

"Hey, boys," he said.

"Glad you're home, sweetheart," Momma said.

He leaned over and gave Momma a kiss. After he sat down, Daddy opened up his paper.

"Listen to this, Allie," he said. "I think Janet Hankley is getting senile." He started to read:

"Raining Green Tomatoes? Mrs. Janet Hankley and her yard man, Hod Burkett, witnessed a strange event this morning. Green tomatoes fell out of the sky . . ." Butch got the giggles, and Daddy stopped reading.

"You boys know something about this? Will?" he said, looking at me real stern.

"It was kind of a joke," I told him. "We made us this giant slingshot out of some old bicycle inner tubes. We hiked down to the ridge and shot some green tomatoes towards the Hankley house. They didn't hurt nothing. They just rolled up on the yard, but we were so far away, Mrs. Hankley and the yard man couldn't tell where they were coming from. They got kind of excited."

"Will Jennison!" Daddy said glaring at me. "If you two boys don't beat all for getting up to mischief." He looked at Momma who was trying to keep a straight face. She covered her mouth with her hands, but she was starting to shake.

Finally, she kicked out her legs, grabbed her sides, and started to hoot with laughter. She laughed so hard she slid down in her chair and tears were rolling down her cheeks.

"Sorry, Frank," she gasped. "Can't help it. Oh! Mysterious green tomatoes! Oh, Lord . . ." she was off again, giggling and laughing.

"Really, Allie," Daddy said, "you shouldn't laugh when these boys do something like this." I could see he was trying hard not to grin. "What if one of those tomatoes had hit Janet Hankley...'Hankley Felled By Falling Tomato'! Huh!"

Now Daddy covered his mouth and started to shake. "Ha! Oh, Lord!" He slid down in his chair and started to laugh, too. Me and Butch joined in with considerable relief. We rolled around on the linoleum and laughed until our stomachs hurt and then we pulled our knees up and held our stomachs and laughed some more. Every time we'd calm down somebody would start it up again.

Lord knows how long this went on, but it was one of the all-time best laughs we ever did have.

Chapter Nine

Johnny

I WOKE UP the next morning with Hooter licking my face. Linc was starting a fire in the stove and putting on the coffee pot. At first I couldn't figure where I was, but then I saw Linc and got it straight.

"Mornin', Linc," I said, sitting up on the quilts. "Mornin', Johnny. After I gets this fire lit we gon' to have some break-fast. Oo-wee! You is one dirty boy." He handed me a chunk of soap. "Go on over to that little beach and clean up, while I fix us something. I was you, I wash out them clothes, too. Like I showed you, that little path gon' off to the lef' go to the out-house. Cut yo' eyes 'round fo' snakes."

I got my extra pair of pants out of my blanket roll and headed for the beach. Hooter ran ahead of me, and when I got to the beach, she was walking around in the water look-ing for fish. She snapped at one, came up empty and stood there with a wet face looking puzzled.

After I cleaned up and washed my clothes and wrung 'em out, I dove back in and floated around on my back. The water was just barely cool, and it felt real silky. There was just a little current, and a couple of strokes now and then kept me next to the beach. I could have stayed there all morning, but I got to thinking about breakfast. I got out and jumped up and down to shake off some of the water and pulled on my clean clothes. When I got back to the house, I smelled the catfish stew and the corn cakes, and I knew I wouldn't have no trouble eating the same meal all over again. Linc looked at me grinning.

"Hee, hee! Lord, Lord…they was a boy under that dirt. After falling 'round in that mud yesterday, Linc gon' have to do some washing, too."

I started in on the catfish stew. "Linc, this is even better than last night," I told him.

"Stews is like that," he said. "All them things needs time to blen' up together." He poured the last of it in my bowl, and I finished it up. Then he poured me a cup of coffee and put in a spoonful of brown sugar. It was strong stuff. Linc was smoking his pipe and having his coffee.

"Put hair on yo' chest, Johnny," he told me.

We took the dishes down to the river where Linc had an old sink nailed on the dock. He left me to do the dishes and headed for the beach to take a bath. I dipped up some river water into the sink and got busy. It took awhile to get the pots and dishes clean. When I brought 'em to the house I seen that Linc was back from the beach. We hung our wet clothes on the porch railing to dry and went on in the house.

After we put up the dishes, and both of us had been to the outhouse, Linc said he was goin' to teach me how to row. Hooter looked mighty sad when we got into the skiff, and she followed along the shoreline, keeping us in sight as long as she could. Linc made rowing look so easy, but when he let me

try. I seen it weren't. Still, with him telling me what to do,
after about a half hour, I started to get the hang of it. 'Bout
the time I was getting the hang of it, he made me stop so I
wouldn't pull blisters on my hands.

We had worked our way out to the main river and the
boat was moving with the current. "Johnny, we gon' drop
down to the bait store an get us some supplies. We can get
some groceries there. I can't feed a boy the same way I eats.
It ain't good enough. I aims to put some meat on yo' bones.
Got to have me some more stuff.

"They's an old man run that store...Mr. Jakes. He purty
nice but mighty curious. I gon' tell him you Mr. Webb's nephew. That you staying with me fo' a while to do some fishin'. I
gon' say you's called Johnny Webb; that way, he won't ask no
questions."

"That's fine with me, Linc. I sure don't want to be called
Brasher no more." I had swapped the money over to my clean
pants, and I reached inside my pants and unsnapped the pin
and took out the five one-dollar bills.

"If I'm going to be livin' off you for a while, Linc, I want to
help pay for what I eat. Sarah give me these five one dollar
bills. You take two of 'em, and I'll keep the rest for when I
have to move on. OK?"

"That's mighty helpful, Johnny. I appreciates it. We can
buy a heap of stuff with this."

When we came around a bend, I saw an old shack built
right out on the river with a dock in front. We tied up the
skiff and went inside. There was a little bit of everything in
that store. There were screen cages full of crickets, a big gal-
vanized tank with minnows in it, and bins of dirt with worms
in 'em. It smelled powerful in there, like an animal cage.

Mr. Jakes could have been fifty or seventy years old. His face was so covered up with gray and white whiskers, you couldn't tell what was underneath. The whiskers around his mouth was all brown from tobacco juice, and, every once in a while, he'd pick up a tin can and spit in it. After he heard I was Mr. Webb's nephew, he didn't pay me no mind except to tease Linc. Wanted to know how an old swamp rat could be turned into a nursemaid. I felt embarrassed when he said that, but Linc said:

"This here boy don' need no nursin'. He take care of hisself jes' fine." We piled groceries in the skiff. Linc even got some fresh eggs.

"Country ham and eggs and grits with gravy tomorrow mornin', Johnny. Linc ain't had a fried egg fo' six months. Uh, uh."

On the way back up river, Linc was rowing against the current, so it took us over an hour to get back. Linc kept the boat in close to shore where the current was weakest and pulled the oars like he would never get tired. He said he had rowed so much he didn't pay it no mind. Said he could probably row all day and all night if he had to, and I believe he could have done it.

I wanted to help, but my hands were red and sore from before. Linc said it would take 'em a while to toughen up.

Hooter sang us a song when we pulled up to the dock. Threw her head back and gave out a long, soft howl with her tail thumping away like crazy.

"Tha's why I calls her Hooter," said Linc. "Couldn't have no barkin' dog out here. Folks would hear that and know where I was."

Me and Linc put the groceries up and ate some cheese and crackers for lunch. Linc poured himself a cup of cold coffee left over from breakfast and lit up his pipe. He tipped back in his chair, relaxing while he smoked.

"Get that bait bucket there, Johnny, and look out on the dock. They's a little scoop net out there wif a long handle on it. Go on down to the end of the island past the beach an' see if you can catch us two or three frogs. You git some, put 'em in the bait bucket. We gon' catch us a nice bass or two fo' supper."

"If there's frogs around, I can catch 'em," I bragged. I got the net, and me and Hooter went down the path. I waded into the marsh at the end of the island. It only took me about ten minutes to get three frogs. Hooter caught one, but it must have jumped around in her mouth too much 'cause she gave a big cough and spit it out. When I got back to the dock, Linc was in the skiff with a long cane pole. I climbed in with the bait bucket, and we pushed off.

Linc rowed us up one creek after another 'til I was completely lost. We were sliding through this little creek that was like a tunnel with trees and bushes meeting overhead when all of a sudden we came out into a huge lake. You could see across it, but it was big.

"Dang!" I said. "Look at that."

"This here called 'Lost Lake'," Linc said.

As we drifted out on the lake, a big hawk took off from a limb nearby.

"Osprey," Linc said. "Come in here to fish. He know a good fishin' spot. Ain't many folks knows 'bout this lake," Linc said. "Me an' that osprey and a few mo'. This here be a good bass place. Cain't catch a bass here, you ain't much count."

We rowed around to a place where a tree had fallen into the lake.

"Be real quiet, Johnny. Don't bung nothin' on the boat. We

gon' hook one of these frogs you caught on this here line…gon' ease that frog right over near the tree."

Linc put a frog on the hook and took the cane pole and swung him over near the half-sunk tree. There was three feet of line between the frog and the float, and it bobbed around as the frog tried to swim away. Linc handed me the pole.

"That cork go down clean-under, you count to five and then liff up hard," he said.

Fishing takes waiting, so I was settling down for a wait when I seen the cork was gone!

"…two, three, fo', five…" Linc counted. I heaved up hard. The pole bent double.

"Hung on the bottom," I says.

"Hung on a fish," says Linc, and sure enough, I felt him move.

"Cain't get him up!" I says. "It's a big'un."

"He big," says Linc. "Take yo' time. You get him. Jes' keep him 'way from that tree."

I kept the pressure on and worked him out into the lake, but every time I got him almost up I saw his belly flash as he rolled and headed for the bottom. This went on for some time, but he must have been getting tired. I know'd I was. Finally, I got him to the surface, and Linc got the net under him. When he was in the boat, I know'd it was the biggest fish I ever caught.

"Tha's a nice fish, Johnny. He big enough to fillet. Go 'bout six pound. You done good."

I was shakin' with excitement. Linc took out the hook and put the fish on a stringer and put him in the lake. Linc sat on the floor of the boat and leaned back against the seat and lit his pipe and waited for me to calm down. After awhile I did, and we just lazed there in the sun for a while. We were quiet, and it was real peaceful. The osprey come back. We seen him on the other side of the lake. He dove on the lake feet first and come up with a fish pumping his wings hard to carry the extra weight.

"Nice thing 'bout livin' out here, Johnny. You don't have to get in no hurry."

I stretched back, too, and put my legs over the side of the boat into the water.

"Yes sir, Linc. This is livin'!"

Later that afternoon, I watched Linc fillet the bass and saw the gator come up and get the remains. I was getting used to Hepburn, but I still didn't hang around too close to the edge of that dock. I fed Hooter her pig food.

Linc had been cooking a pot of black-eyed peas for a couple

of hours. I had drug in a bunch of branches from the island for fire wood, and Linc had chopped 'em up. The peas had got done cooking so Linc set 'em aside and put some more wood in the stove. Then he put some lard in a frying pan and put that on the stove. Soon he had salted and peppered the fish and rolled it in corn meal, and it was sizzling and popping in the hot grease. I had thought nothing could top the catfish stew but that fried bass and black-eyed peas done it.

We ate 'til we was bug-eyed. We just sat there for a time, slumped back in our chairs looking at each other.

"Whew!" said Linc. "That took some doin', eatin' all that."

"Mighty good, Linc. I never had no better fish."

We shoved the dishes aside for later. Linc lit his pipe. "Linc, when's that freight train goin' to come by? I got to try to get to Birmingham, sometime." Linc look at me and reached across the table to put his hand on my shoulder.

"I been studyin' on that freight train, Johnny, and I got to tell you somethin'."

"What, Linc?"

"Johnny, Linc ain't goin' to put you on no freight train." "What you mean, Linc?"

"Johnny, they jes' too many bad folks in this here world. They was a man running 'round Savannah killin' people just a few months back. Folks like that don't care if they hurts chil'ren. Fact is, some of 'em likes to hurt chil'ren. Trus' old Linc. They some terrible, sick-in-the-head folks in this world. Them trains is dangerous, too. You just a boy, honey. You lucky you ain't already been hurt. I jes' cain't do it, Johnny. Linc cain't put you on no freight train."

"But what am I goin' to do, Linc? I can't stay here with you for good."

"I know, Johnny. Linc gon' try somethin'. Soon, I wants to go over and check on the Webb plantation. I has the key. They's a telephone over there. I gon' to call Mr. Webb in Savannah and tell him 'bout you. See can he find out 'bout them folks in Birmingham. You say they be called 'Jameson'?"

"I think Sarah said 'Jennison'. My brother's named Will."

"Maybe Mr. Webb can find that Mr. Jennison. Get him on the phone, see if he can help you."

"Linc, I wasn't too happy 'bout gettin' on that freight train. I like stayin' here with you. I ain't never ate so good." "Tha's jes' fine then, Johnny. You stay right here with ol' Linc 'til we studies out where you goin' to go and how you goin' to git there. Maybe tomorrow we go over to the Webb place."

That night we played some checkers, but I was too tired to think, and Linc beat me twice.

"You git on to bed, Johnny," Linc told me. "We do these dishes in the mornin'."

I stumbled over to my stack of quilts and fell out.

"Night, Linc." "Night, honey."

I woke up in the middle of the night from a sound like a animal being hurt. It was a moaning. I thought something was wrong with Hooter. I felt my way over to the table and fumbled around 'til I finally found the matches. I heard Linc holler: "No! No! Please...No!" I got the lamp lit and went over to Linc and put my hand on his shoulder.

"Linc! Wake up!" I shook him. He sat up and looked around like he didn't know where he was. Tears was running down his face. Then he seen me.

"Johnny! Oh, my goodness. Ol' Linc have a dream. Every once in a while, Linc have that dream. 'Bout my daddy."

"What is it, Linc?"

Linc put his forehead on his knees for a minute, then he looked up and wiped the tears off his face with his right hand. He got up and went over and sat at the table.

"Johnny, my momma die when I was ten. Me and Daddy live together in that little house on the Webb plantation. When I was twelve years old, some bad men all dress' up in white sheets...hoods on they heads...come to that house and tuk my daddy off. I ain't never seen him alive no mo'.

"See, my daddy had always live' free. Hunt and fish in the swamp. He was a man. Colonel Webb was the onliest man Daddy call 'sir'. Wouldn't say that to nobody else. Some white-trash folks didn't like the idea of no black man who held his head up. Caught him in town one time and tole him they was gon' to teach him some manners. He jes' walk off. Few nights after that, them men, dress' up in sheets, come 'round, tuk my daddy off...hung him from a tree limb. When they tuk him, Daddy tole me: 'Don't say nothin',' so I keep quiet.

"Colonel Webb come to help us, but he come too late. When he find out what happened, he set down and cry like a baby. Weren't nothin' he could do. He tole folks that if he ever foun' out who was in those sheets, he'd kill 'em hisself. Tuk to wearin' a pistol. There was some folks layin' mighty low for a long while. Old Colonel Webb weren't a man you could trifle wif.

"They was a bunch of them Scaggs, kin to the folks that own the pig farm, that was livin' by the swamp out east of the plantation. I believe some of them was amongst that bunch that tuk my daddy. Cain't be sho ... Well, anyway, I always thought if I hadn't kep' quiet like Daddy tole me, if I'd gon' an' hollered loud enough, somebody at the plantation house might've heard me, and Colonel Webb might could've got there in time to save my Daddy. When I has that dream, it's 'bout those men draggin' off my daddy. I tries to holler, but I can't git no sound out."

"Oh, Linc," I says and put my hand over his. We sat there together for a while.

"Linc all right now, Johnny. That was a long time back." He put his arms around me and give me a hug.

"Go on back to bed now, Johnny. I gon' smoke my pipe for a few minutes." I did what he said. I lay there in the dark looking at the glow from Linc's pipe and listening to the swamp sounds. Frogs and bugs were singing. I got to thinking about how I felt at night when I was at Aunt Min's, when I was little and used to cry myself to sleep at night.

"Linc?" I said.

"What, Johnny?"

"I wonder if those Jennisons will want me. Maybe they won't want me."

"Honey, they already try to adopt you. Those folks want Will. It's for sho they gon' to want you."

"It's funny, Linc. I don't hardly remember Will, but I miss him. What do you reckon he's like?"

"He like you, Johnny."

Right before I went back to sleep I heard this ol' owl hooting up in the swamp.

"Linc?" I said again. "What, honey."

"It's lonely to lose your folks, ain't it?" "Sho is, honey. Sho is."

Chapter Ten

Will

I WAS BORED. We were having a family dinner that night, so I didn't have a friend over. Momma had gone shopping. Jenny May was busy cooking. Jackson was pushing the carpet sweeper over the rugs. Nobody had any time for me. I had spent the morning reading and hanging around. I found some National Geographic magazines and had been poking through them looking for naked women. I found some, but their necks had been stretched out about a foot long by a bunch of metal rings, which is kind of distracting when you're trying to see naked women.

It was hot. I went out on the pavilion with my slingshot and was shooting rocks trying to hit an old hickory tree that was way down the hill in the woods. Charlie, our golden retriever, was flopped out on the linoleum with his tongue hanging out. I lay down and used Charlie as a pillow. Boring. Then I saw it was getting dark. I sat up.

There were some really fantastic black clouds filling up the valley, rolling around on top of each other taking up more and more of the sky. Thunder started to rumble and

I could see the lightning coming down under the blackest part of the storm. A real humdinger, and it was moving in fast. It got darker still. A cool blast of wind hit me, and the trees began to toss. The summer heat was gone, and the air smelled wet and fresh. It made me feel like I could fly, and I spread my arms and leaned into the wind. I could see the rain coming up the valley in huge, lashing sheets, and there was a blue-white flash that lit up the pavilion and a terrific bang. I saw a bolt of lightning strike the same tree I had been shooting at. I stripped off down to underpants and took my clothes and book to the table in the middle of the pavilion then went back to the railing just as the rain hit.

It came lashing in on me so hard it stung. Yahoo! I yelled and spun around to let the rain get my back, too. Some of the trees were bending like they would surely break. Then I heard Jenny May hollering at me to come in, and I grabbed my clothes and book and ran to the house.

"Lord have mercy, boy, ain't you got no sense? You want to git struck by lightnin'? Yo' momma skin us both alive if she knew you was out there in this storm."

"Ain't it a beauty, Jenny May? Best storm this summer. Bet you Johnny would love this storm. What a beauty!" Jenny May just shook her head.

"Beauty? Lord, chile, you is somethin' else!"

⁓⌐

I put on some clean shorts and a clean shirt but no shoes 'cause I knew we were goin' to eat on the pavilion. I had washed my face real good because I knew my grandmother would fuss if it was dirty. When I went out to the library, Momma checked me over.

"You look clean for a change, Will," she said, giving me a pat. "Did you take a bath?"

"I had a shower," I told her, but I didn't mention that it was a rain shower.

———◦

Daddy was listening to the console radio, looking disgusted as he usually did when he heard the news. Charlie started barking his head off at the screen door as Judge pulled his car up in front of the house. I heard the car doors close and heard my grandparents coming up the stone steps to the front door.

"Hush up, Charlie," Judge said. "Lord, what a racket!" He held open the door for my grandmother. Her name was Sophie, and that's what we all called her, even me and Janie and Henry.

"Hey, honey," Sophie said to me, when I went to the door. She put her finger to her lips and slipped me a chocolate bar. Both my grandparents gave me a kiss.

Judge had on his usual black suit. He had white hair and a white, bristly mustache and always looked kind of red in the face. Judge seemed fierce, but Sophie was plump and sweet-looking. She was a fresh, well-powdered Southern lady, but her hair and dresses usually seemed like they didn't quite know where they ought to be. She smiled a lot and had the twinkliest eyes.

"Frank, you hear what that damn fool Roosevelt said?" Judge asked Daddy.

"*Pas devant l'enfant,* Judge," Sophie said. I had long since figured out that meant "Don't cuss in front of the boy."

"Good to see you, sir," Daddy said. "I've just been listening to Roosevelt's latest idea. That man's goin' to ruin the country, if he has enough time." Momma came in and kissed Sophie and Judge.

"Now, Judge," Momma said, "don't you men start on Roosevelt. You know Todd likes him. If you two get in an argument with Todd, the rest of us won't get a word in edgewise."

"OK, honey, no politics…speak of the Devil," he said, as my uncle, Todd, and Aunt Evelyn came in with Janie and Henry following along behind. I loved Momma's younger brother, Todd. He was tall and thin and, unless something got him goin' on politics, he didn't say much. When he did say something, it was generally funny. He was a reporter for the Birmingham News. He was a hero to me. He had flown for the British in the war and had shot down several German planes.

The trouble with family parties is all the kissing. Grownups are something awful for kissing. It went on and on 'til they finally got worn out with it. Us kids were ducking and wiping spit off. I went up to Janie.

"That's a mighty pretty dress you got on, Janie," I said, pointing at the old green overalls she had on. That made her mad, and she jumped on me. I tripped, and we both went down. I was laughing so hard it made me weak. She grabbed me by the ears and started banging my head on the floor. Good thing we were on the carpet. Uncle Todd pulled her off.

"What's goin' on here, you two?"

"He made fun of my overalls, Daddy."

"Well, good gracious, Janie, that's no reason to knock his head off."

"She couldn't hurt me, Uncle Todd. She's just a girl." Janie jumped me again and Uncle Todd pulled her off.

"Now cut it out, you two," he said like he meant it.

"Shake hands." We shook hands and Janie made a face.

We went out on the pavilion where there were cocktails for the grown-ups and ice tea for us kids. After we all sat down, Momma told them about Mrs. Hankley and the green tomatoes. When everybody quit laughing, Judge started in telling an amazing dog story, which I had heard many times. It was about a little mongrel dog named Plim he had had as a boy.

"…anyway," Judge was saying, "that Plim was an adventurer. We lived just up the street from the fire station and, you know, in those days there were nothing but horse-drawn fire engines. Flim loved to go to fires. When he heard fire-engine bells clanging, he would run down to Highland Avenue and crouch by the side of the road. He'd run along just behind the horses and, at just the right instant, he'd make his move. He'd jump between the nearest horse and the engine and grab the horses tail in his mouth. That fool dog would ride to the fire swinging in the air off the horse's tail.

"It was the most daredevil thing I ever saw. One false move and he would have been crushed by the fire engine. We saw him do that many times and he never got hurt."

"Wonder why he liked fires so much?" asked Aunt Evelyn, who was tall and beautiful but kind of in her own world.

"It wasn't the fire he liked," said Judge, "it was getting there. Come to think of it, the journey usually is better than getting somewhere."

"Frank," Todd said, "Evelyn has been telling me something about your trying to find Will's twin brother. What's goin' on?" Daddy told everybody what had happened.

"If that doesn't beat all!" Sophie said. "That poor child! We've got to do something about that boy."

"We've got to find him first," said Daddy. "What if you do find him?" Aunt Evelyn said.

"We'll try to adopt him," Momma told her. "We tried before, but the aunt took him."

"Yeah, well, you might have a problem there," Judge said. "'Course that's Tennessee law, but if that aunt tries to hang on to him, you might have a problem."

"But the woman mistreated him," Momma said. "We know that for a fact."

"I know, honey," Judge said. "But boys have been switched before and sent to bed without supper."

"Not every night, Daddy."

"I'm just saying that if that Brasher woman wants to hang on to the boy, you might have a problem."

"Judge, the woman doesn't want the boy," Daddy told him. "She said so. Besides, she's insane. I talked to her less than a minute, and the woman was positively frothing at the mouth, cursing…she's crazy…no doubt about it."

"Exactly," Judge said. "Somebody who's crazy with meanness will do things to spite you. If she thinks you want the boy, she'll probably try to keep him, and the law will be on her side. I'm not saying you can't get the boy, Frank; I'm just saying it may not be easy."

"Well, we just have to take it one step at a time," Daddy said. "First of all, we've got to find Johnny. Like I said, he's disappeared. Will feels he's all right, and sometimes a twin can sense such a thing. We just have to wait and see if we can find out where he is. We'll worry about Mrs. Brasher after we find him."

"I bet somebody has taken him in and is looking after him," Momma said.

"A colored man," I said.

"What makes you think that, son?" Daddy asked me. "Last night I had this dream," I said. "In the dream, Johnny was walking on some boards. A colored man was walking behind him with his hand on Johnny's shoulder." Everybody looked at me.

~~~

We were too full of corn pudding, garden tomatoes, green beans, biscuits and fried chicken to play tag, and, besides, it

wasn't much fun with only three kids and with Henry too
chubby to run fast. We got us a jar and started catching lightning bugs. As the darkness fell, they came out by the hundreds. Soon we had fifty or so in the jar and we came over and
flopped in the grass near where the grown-ups were talking.
Their voices droned on and on. Uncle Todd must have been
watching us lying there in the green glow of the lightning bugs.

"Something strange happened to me when I was a boy," he
said. "I never told this to anyone before, and I don't know if
youall will believe me, but it really happened. I was sitting on
our porch looking towards the woods watching fireflies—lots
of 'em, like tonight—when all of a sudden, all of these hundreds and hundreds of fireflies started to blink on-and-off at
the same time. It went on like that for some time. On, off, on,
off…all of 'em, perfectly synchronized. I never told anybody.
It was too unbelievable."

"My, my…" said Sophie. "Dearie me…."

I rolled onto my back and put my hands under my head.
My family's conversation washed over me soft and familiar
as the sweet-smelling evening air. I was wishing Johnny was
there. That would make everything right.

A shooting star streaked across the sky….

Chapter Eleven

Johnny

*T*HE NEXT MORNING Linc had a fire goin' when I woke up. He put a pot of grits and the coffee pot on the stove, and we went over to the little beach with Hooter to wash up. After we soaped up and rinsed off, we floated there and watched the sunrise. The sky lit up all gold and a flight of birds come over. I never seen anything so white. Linc said they was white ibis heading for Lost Lake. After a little while, Linc told me:

"Hop on out now, Johnny, snake comin'." I climbed out in a hurry and, sure enough, here come a big old snake curling through the water. "Brown water snake, Johnny. He ain't got no poison, but he mean. Bite you five, six times jes' fo' the fun of it. Mos' snakes scoot off an' try to git away from you, but not him. No, suh. He come git you like a mean dog. Old Hooter got her nose all bit up one time. She don' sniff no snakes no mo'." Hooter was watching the snake with considerable respect.

We headed on back to the cabin, and Linc got a ham down off a hook and started cutting slices. The swim had made us hungry, and we had us a humdinger of a breakfast. Linc made us some more corn cakes and then used the same griddle to fry up the ham and eggs, and that ham smelled so good it was hard to wait for it. He put some water on the griddle and simmered up some red-eye gravy that he put on the grits. We dug into the ham and eggs and grits and sopped up gravy and egg yolk with them corn cakes. "Good" ain't the word for it. After we had some coffee, done the dishes, and visited the outhouse, Linc said, "Come on, honey, we gon' check up on Mr. Webb place."

We got in the skiff, and Linc poled us out to the river. He took us out a different way. Twisty channels through deep swamp. Yes, sir, I was lost again. We come around a bend in the channel and found three gators laying in the sun up on a mud bank. As we come up, two of 'em slid in the water, but the other one, a big old bull, stood on his toes and hissed at us. It was fearsome, but we slid on past, and he settled back down. We passed another island, and I wanted to climb up on it and look around. Linc said it was a "floater," made out of peat. He poked the edge of the island with his pole and, sure enough, you could see it wobble and shake. He said you could walk on a floater but sometimes your legs would punch through and you'd sink down in muddy peat up to your tailbone. When that happened, he said, you most generally come up with leeches on your legs. Said it was easy to step on a gator, too, walking around on a floater. Didn't sound like near as much fun as I had thought. Link pointed to a watery trail goin' through a grassy flat.

"Gator nest up there, Johnny. Big ol' pile of mud and straw where that gator lay her eggs. Don' want to mess with no gator nest. Momma gator, she don' take kindly to it."

When we reached the river, Linc pushed us out in the current, which started to carry us along at a pretty good clip.

I was trailing my feet in the water and Linc sat on the bottom of the boat resting his elbows on the seat and smoking.

"Might as well res' now," he said. "Gon' to have to work gettin' home."

"When we come back, I can row some," I says. "Sho," says Linc.

We floated down the river with the boat spinnin' around real slow. It was quiet; nothing but deep swamp on both sides. Now and then, I'd hear a bird or a frog up in the swamp. The cypress trees was spooky looking...hung with moss. Bright sun was on the banks, but ten feet back in the swamp it was all dark and mysterious. Linc pointed out a wildcat with his front feet in the water, drinking; and, one time, I seen a otter laying on his back on a floating log eating a fish like it was corn on the cob. Linc said there was all kind of critters in the swamp, even black bears.

"Critters do fine in the swamp," he said, "but if a man want to live in the swamp he got to have him a boat and a way to keep the skeeters off at night."

We drifted on for quite a ways 'til finally we come around a bend in the river where the swamp opened up to some grass flats.

"Look yonder," Linc said.

Up past the flats on some high ground stood a huge house. It was grayish-white like an old ghost looming up amongst the trees. Great big windows and columns across the front. The oak and cypress trees had moss hanging down, and one tree, with shiny, dark green leaves, had white flowers as big as saucers.

"Looks haunted, Linc."

"Well...Linc don't know 'bout no ghosts, but they's a heap

a memories hanging round that ol' place. I growed up there, out back, in that little house, like I tole you. My momma and daddy's buried near there. Colonel Webb, he put up a nice stone on Daddy's grave. I gon' show you."

We tied the boat to the dock and walked up the board walkway to the yard.

"Uh oh." Linc said. "What?"

"Somebody been here." Linc got down on one knee to look at some footprints. "Hasn't been too long. Rain heavy three nights back. Been since then." We went up to the house and walked all around it.

"Everything look all right," Linc said. "Ain't nobody broke in. Man done walk all 'round, though. Look in all the windows. Come on, Johnny," Linc pulled out the key. "Le's go on in."

Inside, the house was amazing. I hadn't never seen nothing like it. Mr. Webb had kept it in good shape. Shiny floors. Huge rooms. Rich-colored carpets. Window drapes. Linc said they was silk. Fancy-looking old furniture. Linc called them antiques.

There was a dining room with a big ol' table with lots of chairs around it. There was beautiful, silver candle sticks and silver bowls and such in there. One big old room was a library, just crammed with books.

"Linc, you could spend your life in here and never read your way through all these books."

"Honey, Linc couldn't read his way through one of 'em."

"My gosh, Linc, can't you read?"

"Not a word, honey. Ol' Linc never learn to read. Colored

folks ain't gon' to no school back when I was a boy."

"Linc, you been teachin' me all kind of things; now there's somethin' I can teach you."

"Reckon you could, Johnny? Linc purty ol' to learn to read. Sho would like to solve that mystery."

"You could, Linc. It's easy once you get the hang of it. I can show you. It'll be more fun than playin' checkers. Could we borrow some of these books?"

"Sho, Johnny. You get some. Mr. Webb won't mind. He give 'em to you if you was to ask fo' 'em."

I went to poking through the books while Linc tried to telephone Mr. Webb. I found a shelf full of children's books and pulled out some that I thought would be good for Linc to learn on. Linc came back in the library.

"Mr. Webb in Europe, Johnny. Won't be back fo' two weeks. Looks like you stuck wif Linc a while longer."

"I ain't in no hurry, Linc," I told him. "That'll give us time to get you started reading."

"Johnny, we got to spend some time over here at the plantation. We gon' to move over here and sleep fo' a few nights."

"Why, Linc?"

"That man what lef' them tracks 'round the house...he might come back. He might want to get in...steal stuff. Mr. Webb trus' me to be lookin' after this place."

"Couldn't it have been a curious fisherman, Linc?" "Could have, Johnny, but I don' think so. I seen where he spit tobacco. Tha's mo' like one of these local folks. I seen some knife marks 'round one of the window latches. Give me the idea somebody studyin' on breakin' in. Le's get gon'. We got a heap of stuff to do."

It was an hour hard rowing to get back to Linc's place. I took a turn and was getting better at it. We loaded up supplies: food, the lantern, extra clothes, food for Hooter who was coming back with us...all the little odds and ends that Linc thought we would need. Before we left the house, Linc took up his shotgun and a handful of shells.

"Double-aught buckshot, Johnny. Linc ain't fixin' to let nothin' happen to you."

When we got back to the plantation it was late afternoon. We unloaded our stuff on the dock, and Linc took the boat and hid it up a little creek he knew about. We set up camp in the front hall downstairs. Linc brought down a couple of mattresses and we put 'em near the front door and put our clothes and stuff on the floor nearby. We ate some ham and cheese and crackers and I seen it was getting dark. There was electricity in the plantation house, but it was shut off. Linc didn't want any light to show outside so he left the lantern in the library and pulled the drapes across the windows. He went out and walked around to see if any light was showing. Finally, we settled down at the desk with some books and the lantern to read by.

"Gone be stuffy in here," Linc said.

"How we goin' to know if he sneaks up on the house, Linc?"

"Ain't nobody gon' sneak up on Hooter," Linc said." He had left Hooter in the front hall, where some windows were open.

Well, nothing happened that first night. We stayed in the library and I went over the alphabet with Linc. He already know'd most of the letters, so I mainly showed him how to sound 'em out like I'd been showed in school. After a couple of hours, I got sleepy, so we went in the front hall and stretched out on the mattresses. Hooter lay down between us, and I reached over and scratched her ear. We had left some side windows open, and there was a little breeze coming in off the river.

"Linc, ain't it strange to be layin' here in the dark in this big ol' house?"

"Mighty strange, honey."

The second day Linc showed me the little house where he grew up. It was a small log cabin all boarded up and mostly covered with vines. Out behind the house he showed me his parent's graves. There was a small stone on his momma's grave that said: "Julia Fraiser, 1863–1893". The larger stone said: "Joshua Fraiser, Honorable man, loved and trusted friend, 1847–1895." Then he showed me the little house his parents had owned.

"Linc, ain't you never been married?"

"I has Johnny, befo' I move in the swamp. Me and my wife live in Savannah. I was workin' on the fishin' boats. We had us a little girl. She die when she was three from the typhoid. 'Bout a year after that, my wife run off wif a good-lookin' gambler from Chicago. Never seed her no more. 'Bout then, Linc think he do better livin' on his own. Mr. Webb ask me if I move back to the plantation. Be his caretaker. I live in this same little house fo' three years 'til I built my little place in the swamp."

"You sure have had some hard luck, Linc," I told him. "Yes, Lord. Linc done had his share, but look now, honey, I got three good friends…Mr. Webb, you, and Hooter."

"I hope we'll always be friends, Linc." "You can count on me, honey."

⁓

The next day we were settin' on the front porch working on reading when Hooter started to whine. Linc looked up.

"Boat comin'. Le's get on inside."

We went in and watched the dock from one of the front windows near our mattresses. We heard a small outboard motor getting closer. It stopped. Pretty soon we seen somebody coming up towards the house on the boardwalk.

"Oh, Lord!" said Linc. "That look like Bobby Scagg, the worstest Scagg they is. He drunk. Johnny, you stay in the house." I backed up into the dark room where I couldn't be seen and watched out the open front door.

Linc picked up the shotgun which was broke and slid two shells into it. They made funny, hollow clicks like dropping rocks into a glass jug. He went out on the porch with Hooter and down the front steps. Bobby Scagg was coming up the walk. He was lean and tough-looking with big knobby hands hanging out of his work shirt. His eyes were bloodshot, and there was tobacco juice at the corners of his mouth. He had a old felt hat pushed back and long greasy blond hair hung around his face, which was red from sunburn and drinking.

"What you lookin' fo', Mr. Scagg?" Linc asked him. "None-a-yer damn business!" he said.

"Bes' you go on home, Mr. Scagg. This here private property. You knows I be Mr. Webb caretaker. I cain't let nobody be messin' roun' this place."

"You ain't no damn caretaker. Yer jest a nigger. Git out-ta my way." He started towards Linc. Linc snapped the gun shut, and Hooter started a low, rumbling growl.

"No, suh," Linc said. Bobby Scagg stopped.

"You gonna shoot me, boy? Nigger shoot a white man?

Gimme that goddam gun." He made another move to-wards Linc, and Hooter went for him. He tried to run, but Hooter got a hold of his boot, and down he went. Linc called off Hooter.

"Bes' go on home, Mr. Scagg."

"I'll git you fer this, nigger. I got a gun in my boat."

"Mr. Scagg, I ain't never shoot nobody befo', but you come off that dock wif a gun, I reckon I gon' do it. This here dou-ble-aught buckshot, Mr. Scagg. You bes' go on home."

"I'll be back, nigger."

"No, suh. Bes' not to come back here. I gon' have a talk wif the sheriff. He know I work fo' Mr. Webb. Any kind of trouble roun' this house, he gon' know where to come lookin'.'"

Bobby Scagg stood there breathing hard for quite a while. His hands was hanging down by his sides, and his fingers curled up slow into fists. His mouth was in a kind of twisted sneer and his eyes were narrowed to slits. Without taking his eyes off Linc, he spit a stream of tobacco juice towards him. He raised his fist and opened his finger and jabbed it at Linc.

"You ain't got no idea what yer up ag'in." He was spitting out the words, hissing like a evil-looking snake. "Us Scaggs know how to fix proud niggers. Did you know my pa hung a nigger on a tree limb once. Nigger called Fraiser. How you like 'at? Now, you listen up real good. I'm gonna fix you, too. I know you live up in the swamp, and I know just about where. Some dark night soon, I'm goin' ter find where yer at and yer gonna burn. Think on that, nigger!"

He turned and staggered back towards the dock. We heard the motor start up. After a little while, the sound faded out on up the river. Linc unloaded the gun and came in the house and sunk down on the mattress. He looked old and tired. He put his head in his hands and let out a long shuddery sigh. "Lord, Johnny. I always thought them Scaggs had somethin' to do wif killin' my daddy. Now I knows it fo' sho. Lord God, that man goin' cause me grief."

"Can he find your place, Linc?"

"He won' quit 'til he do. Uh, uh. Johnny, we gon' have to stay on our toes. Just to be on the safe side, we gon' hide the boat when we gits back. Then, no matter what happen, we got us a way to get out of the swamp. Good thing we got Hooter. Like I tol' you…cain't nobody sneak up on Hooter." I believed it. I'd seen it.

While I started carryin' our stuff to the boat, Linc got on

the telephone and told the sheriff about Bobby Scagg. After a few minutes, he come along down to the dock with the last of our stuff.

"Sheriff gon' stop by here now and then," he told me. "I don' think Bobby Scagg be comin' roun' here no mo'. We needs to git on back. We just 'bout out of food. We gon' check that fishin' line on the way back."

"Did you tell the sheriff about me, Linc?" I asked him. "I didn't say nothin' 'bout you, Johnny. Police be funny. Likes to take charge. I don' want nobody but Mr. Webb takin' charge of you, honey."

We put the mattresses back, got our stuff together and locked the place up.

"It's a mighty fine house, Linc," I said, "but I like your place better."

"Me, too, Johnny. Let's us get on home."

Chapter Twelve

Will

*L*ORD, THAT summer drug.

Butch had gotten a part time job delivering newspapers on his bicycle and hadn't been able to come over much. Waiting to hear something about Johnny was getting on our nerves. Momma wasn't herself at all. She had even snapped at me a couple of times when I'd bothered her. Daddy's work had piled up on him at the office, and he had told me that he was goin' to have to skip our morning rides for a while so that he could get to the office early. A couple of days before that, Momma had gotten a telephone call from the Birmingham chief of police saying that a boy's body had been found near the tracks up near Jasper. Momma got real upset and called Daddy, and he went to see if it was Johnny. It turned out to be the body of a blond-headed boy...the child of a coal miner. The boy had most likely been trying to jump on a moving freight train and fallen on the tracks. I was sorry about the child getting killed but awful glad it wasn't Johnny. Two days later something else sad happened.

Momma had gone shopping and Jackson had taken the

station wagon to the store to get groceries. Jenny May was
getting supper ready.

I had been down near the woods where the hillside was
mostly bare rock. I had my slingshot and was looking for
rattlesnakes and this time I found one, a big one, coiled up
and looking like it wanted me to come a little closer. Usually
snakes will try to get away from you, but this one didn't. I
had time to load my slingshot with four rusty, iron nuts. I
pulled back and let fly. I got him! I hit him just behind the
head. He was wiggling and flopping around 'til I got a big
rock and finished him off. That snake was long as I was and
big around as my upper arm. He had eleven rattles.

Nobody was home but Jenny May, and I was looking for-
ward to showing off my snake. Not everybody gets a five-
foot rattlesnake with a slingshot. I carried him up to the
screen porch.

Jenny May was sitting there shelling peas. She had a
whole bowl full of them in her lap. I made a mistake.

"Look here, Jenny
May," I said, feeling real
proud. I held the snake
up to the screen next to
where she was sitting.

"Eeeeeee! Eeeeeee!
Eeeeeeeeeeee!" There
was an explosion of
green peas, and Jenny
May disappeared into
the kitchen.

"Oops!" I said out
loud. I had forgotten how

Jenny May felt about snakes. I went down to the edge of the woods and took out my pocket knife and cut off the rattles. I left the snake there, so I could show him to Daddy who would be more likely to appreciate him.

After all the excitement, I was ready to settle down on the daybed with my book. I was on my own. Jenny May had gone down to her little house to stretch out and recover from her shock. I got my book and headed for the screen porch. I was reading some scary stories by Edgar Allen Poe. There was a thunderstorm building and the sky was getting real dark. I heard Momma's car pull up and saw her run in the house to start closing windows. I went and helped her, and when we finished, I brought my book into the living room and stretched out on the sofa under the big picture window where there was still some light. It was getting darker and darker in the house, and I was really getting in the mood. I was reading a story called "The Telltale Heart," and my heart was goin' faster than usual. I read the rest of the story. The air had gotten real still like it does just before a storm, and I heard a funny sound like sobbing. I put down my book and went towards the sound. It was coming from the hall that led to Momma and Daddy's room. I went to their door. It sounded like she was in there crying.

I opened the door. "Momma?"

The room was dark, and she was sitting on the bed sobbing as if her heart would break. "Momma, what's the matter?" She couldn't talk. I snapped on the lights and saw that there were boxes on the floor and baby clothes on the bed. I held her hand.

"Momma, what is it? Don't cry. What is it?" She began to stop. She patted my hand.

"I'm all right, sweetheart. It's just these...these baby clothes. Will...I had a baby...before you came to us. There was something wrong with her heart.

"She...she died when...when she was three months old. I...thought I would give these clothes away, but they...they..." She started to cry again, only quieter. I patted her hand, and after a while she stopped.

"Will,...after I had the baby, the doctor told me that I couldn't have any...more. Any more...babies."

"Is that why you adopted me?" I asked her. She hugged me.

"Yes, sweetheart," she hugged me, "it turned out to be a blessing in disguise. It's just these clothes. They brought back so many...memories. It was a very sad time for me and your daddy." I patted her hand. We just sat there for a few minutes while she stopped crying and blew her nose.

"Momma, let me put these clothes in the boxes. I'll give the boxes to Jackson. You go get a glass of ice tea." She gave me a quick smile.

"I'll take you up on that, sweetie." After she left, I packed up the clothes. The little dresses and all were so tiny. I hadn't known that babies were that tiny. I took the boxes to the porch. The storm had missed us. The sun was out again. I saw Momma coming back from the kitchen through the dining room.

"Will, where's Jenny May? There are peas all over the back porch."

"Uh, well...see...I...uh.... It's hard to explain." "Try."

"Well,...I was down in the woods with my slingshot, and I, uh...I killed this huge rattlesnake, see...I...uh, wanted to show it to somebody."

"Yes . . ."

"I guess I wasn't thinking too good, Momma. I, uh, I kind of held it up a little too close to the screen. Jenny May was sitting there shelling peas, and…"

"Oh, brother!" Momma said, shaking her head and starting to grin.

Chapter Thirteen

Johnny

ME AND LINC ain't had as much fun after that time at the plantation. We was worried. Who wouldn't be? That Bobby Scagg was pure mean. We was afraid to leave the house. We was afraid that if we went off too far, we'd come back an find the house burnt. Linc said Bobby Scagg was a coward and wouldn't come in the daytime, but we daren't risk it. We only went off far enough to fish for dinner.

There was fish all up in that swamp, and Linc knew how to catch 'em. Linc had dried red beans, and some nights we just had red beans with rice with country ham cooked in it. Linc always knew how to come up with a tasty dinner even when the pickin's was slim. I never know'd a better cook.

Most days, we just sat out on the dock and worked on Linc's reading. It was August and plenty steamy in that swamp. Sometimes, there'd be a touch of breeze coming off the grass flats, and the dock, which was mostly in the shade, was the best place to catch it. Linc was getting right good at reading. I was showing him how to form letters, so he'd be able to write. We didn't have no pencils, so we used charred pieces of wood from the ashes out of the cooking stove. There were a few boards on the dock that were smooth enough to write on, and when we filled those up, I'd scoop up some water out of the creek and wash 'em off. When they dried, we'd start all over. Sometimes we'd scoop up the creek water and pour it over ourselves to cool off. The cool would last about fifteen minutes, and then we'd have to do it all over again. We'd been living like this for about two week, trying to keep cool and studying.

"Johnny, this here English langrige sho be funny. Don't make no sense that a word that start with a K gon' soun' like 'no'. I knows 'know' be 'no', but I don' like it."

"Yeah, it's strange, ain't it?" I said. "I'm used to it, but when I stop to think about it, it does seem strange."

It was surprising how much Linc could do. He was reading and getting more and more excited about it. When I was goin' to sleep, he'd still be up trying to puzzle out a paragraph in some book. We went to the beach to bathe, but we never stayed long, and wherever we went, Linc took the shotgun.

Yes, sir, it was a long, slow time. A time of waiting…for trouble.

After two weeks went by, we started to relax. We began to think that Bobby Scagg was all mouth and that nothing was goin' to happen. One morning Linc said:

"Johnny we got to go in fo' supplies. We's scratchin' bottom, honey. We's 'bout out of rice and coffee…and Linc 'bout out of tobacco. We gon' have to take a chance and go see Mr. Jakes tomorrow."

"OK, Linc," I says. "Let's go. If Bobby Scagg ain't come by now, maybe he ain't comin'."

"Tha's right, Johnny, Maybe he ain't," he said, but he looked worried.

That night I was sleeping like a dead man. I woke up with Linc's fingers on my mouth.

"Johnny, be quiet." he whispered. "Somethin' out there."

I was awake in an instant, heart goin' fast. Hooter was whining softly.

"Hush, Hooter. Lay down," Linc whispered and she went quiet. Linc had the shotgun, and we eased out the back door of the little house and snuck up the path on the island. Hooter was between me and Linc and never made a sound. I followed Linc, and after a while, I seen him move off the path through the woods to a place where we could see the creek in front of the house. We sunk down on our knees and then laid down, propped up on our elbows, so we could see under the bushes. The moon was up, so there was some light. I heard a thump and looked and saw a boat sliding up the creek toward the house. I could see someone in the boat with a pole.

That was what had made the thump. I seen him put down the pole and pick up something. The boat had slid up close to the dock. All of a sudden the man struck a match, and I seen what he had in his other hand. It was a whiskey bottle half full of something with a piece of rag stuck in the neck.

"Oh, Lord." Linc whispered. I had my hand on his arm. I could feel his muscles quivering and I felt him shift around as he lifted up the shotgun to his shoulder.

In the light of the match, I could see Bobby Scagg's face, drunk and evil-looking.

He stood there swaying and breathing hard; then, he held the match to the bottle and lit the rag, but gasoline must have leaked out of the bottle when it laid in the bottom of the boat 'cause blue flames run down the side of the bottle and onto Bobby Scagg's right hand.

He let out an angry grunt-like cough and dropped the bottle. It must have fell on something hard in the bottom of the boat and broke, 'cause, before I could think what was happening, that boat was full of fire. There was Bobby Scagg, knee-deep in flames. He screamed and started to do this awful dance in the flames.

Then, he did the only thing he could do: he leapt out of the boat. He hit the creek and went under and, quick as he did, the creek started to churn and boil. It was a hellish sight to see. The burning boat was being tossed around, and weird shadows were dancing over the black water. I seen a leg fly up then something long and black lashed out. The water gave one more heave like there was a underwater explosion, and then I seen some swirls moving down the creek, and the black water settled back flat and glassy in the light of the flames.

Bobby Scagg was gone. My fingers were diggin' in to Linc's arm.

"He...he ..." I couldn't say it. "Gawda'mighty, Linc, he ..." Linc put his hand on my shoulder.

"The garbage man tuk him, Johnny. The garbage man tuk him."

Well, we went on back to the house and lit the lantern. Linc unloaded the shotgun and hung it up. I got a drink from the dipper at the water barrel, and Linc poured himself a cup of cold coffee and lit up his pipe. I could see his hands were shaking.

"Linc, that's about the weirdest thing I ever seen."

"Me, too, Johnny. Linc don't never want to see nothin' like that no mo'."

"You could have shot him, easy, Linc."

"I jes' couldn't, honey. Linc don't want killin' nobody on his conscience, not even Bobby Scagg."

We just sat there for a long while trying to take in what had happened. Finally, Linc gave a long shuddery sigh.

"Lord, Lord! Johnny, we got us a job to do." "What, Linc?"

"We needs to get rid of that boat. We got to pull it out to the river. Turn it loose in the current. That boat fetch up somewhere downstream, way long 'way from here. Somebody fine that boat, it gon' look like Bobby Scagg got drunk and set hisself afire and drown. Come to think on it, tha's jes' 'bout what did happen. You got to come wif me, Johnny. I cain't leave you up in this swamp without no boat. Somethin' happen to Linc...if I couldn't git back...you be stuck."

We were both in our underwear, so we pulled on our clothes and went and got our skiff out of the creek where it was hid and rowed over to Bobby Scagg's boat.

"How come it didn't burn up, Linc?" I asked him.

"That boat ain't got no paint on it. Been sittin' in the water and out in the rain. Done soak up too much water to burn."

Linc was right. When he tied our boat onto the front of Bobby Scagg's boat and started to row, it was so heavy it was hard to get it moving. Once he got it goin', though, it kept on sliding along behind us, and after about a half hour of hard rowing, we come out of the swamp. Linc pulled for the middle of the river where the current was the swiftest. He climbed over me and untied the boat and gave it a push.

"Whiskey bottles in that boat, Johnny. That man must've been some drunk. Onliest way he could git his courage up. Gun in there, too, mostly burnt up."

Linc started to row, and we pulled away from the other boat, which went on down-river, turning slowly in the current.

"Well, that the last we has to think about Bobby Skagg," Linc said. "We can forget about that man. You know, honey, seem to me sooner or later mean folks go down all by they-selves. Gone be mighty restful not havin' to worry....Johnny?"

"What, Linc?"

"I wants to tell you one thing. We got to be careful who we talks to 'bout tonight. Bobby Scagg had him a heap of kin. Them folks ever get the idea Linc had somethin' to do with the end of Bobby Scagg, the truth wouldn't make no difference."

"I understand, Linc. Don't worry 'bout me."

"You a good boy, Johnny. Linc don't never worry 'bout you. You know, Johnny, I don' believe I gon' be havin' no mo' dreams 'bout what happened to my daddy. It seem like what happen tonight finish up what those men done to my daddy."

We got home about dawn, tied up to the dock and went up to the house. We flopped out with our clothes on. The next thing I know'd, it was nearly noon, and I was sweatin' up a storm. Linc was lighting the stove to make some breakfast. Last night seemed like a bad dream. I got up and stretched.

"Nothin' to worry about today, Linc," I said, grinnin' at him. He came over and took my hands and held them up.

"Nothin' to worry about, Johnny!" He jumped in the air. "Hee, hee, hee! Nothin' to worry about, honey!" We were still holding hands and started to caper around each other like a couple of crazy folks. I started to laugh and so did Linc. "Hee, hee, hee!" We hadn't laughed in a long while.

After breakfast we took Hooter over to the beach and got ourselves cleaned up. We were sweaty and dirty from the night before and some chewed by skeeters, so we lay in the water off the beach and floated, not a care in the world. The water felt wonderful.

That afternoon we headed down-river to Mr. Jakes' store. I could see I wasn't goin' to need the rest of my money so I gave it to Linc for supplies. We stocked up good. We got some more fresh eggs and store-bought bread and some garden vegetables a farmer had brought in. On the way home we checked the trotline and had us another catfish. That night we had a real feed, and did we eat. I guess the worry had been taking our appetites, and we had some catching up to do. After dinner Linc shoved back and lit his corncob pipe.

"We gon' res' up tomorrow, Johnny; but the day after that, we gon' to the plantation and call Mr. Webb. He be back from Europe by now."

"I ain't too happy about leavin' here, Linc," I told him.

"Linc don't like it too much either, honey, but you got to try to find yo' folks."

"They ain't exactly my folks, Linc."

"They gon' to be, honey. You see. Trus' ol' Linc."

Chapter Fourteen

Will

SUNDAY MORNING we had finished a late breakfast. Momma had gotten up to eat with us, but, still, she only had toast and bacon.

"How about a ride, son?" Daddy asked me.

"That would be great!" I told him. The phone rang, and Daddy picked it up.

"Hello."

"…Who?"

"…Right, Mr. Webb. This is Frank Jennison. What can I do for you?"

"…Yes, sir, that's right. We did adopt a boy named Will. Yes, sir, he has red hair and freckles." He listened and then covered the phone with his hand and turned to us.

"He knows where Johnny is," he whispered.

"...Excuse me, Mr. Webb. Go ahead." He listened some more.

"...Yes, we've been looking for Johnny Brasher."

Daddy told him all about adopting me and why they hadn't been able to adopt Johnny, too. Then he told him about me seeing Johnny from the train and what had happened since we had been trying to find him. Mr. Webb must have asked Daddy what he did for a living 'cause Daddy told him he was the vice president of the L&N Railroad. Then Daddy listened and covered the phone again and whispered to us:

"He's in land and timber. Has a plantation northwest of Savannah."

Then Daddy told Mr. Webb that Johnny had been mistreated and that he and Momma wanted to try to get custody of Johnny and adopt him. After he finished explaining all this, Daddy listened for quite a while.

"...I understand, Mr. Webb. That's very kind of you. We would have to leave today. Reservations may be a problem. May I call you back?"

"...Yes, I'll call within the hour. Many thanks, Mr. Webb. Good bye, sir." He turned to us.

"Johnny's all right. Evidently, the boxcar that Johnny climbed on got shunted over to Georgia and dropped on a siding in the middle of nowhere. He was found by a colored man named Linc Fraiser, who works as a caretaker for Mr. Webb. Looks after his plantation house. The plantation is on the edge of a big swamp called Blackwater Swamp about a hundred miles from Savannah. Linc Fraiser has a house way up in the swamp. That's where he took Johnny. Your dream about a colored man looking after Johnny was right on the money, son."

"Momma slumped down in her chair, looking stunned. "My God, Frank, no wonder we couldn't find him!" she said.

"Yeah, he's been way up in a swamp." Daddy said. "Linc Fraiser has been looking after the boy and trying to reach Mr. Webb, but Webb has been traveling. Been in Europe. Yesterday, Fraiser finally got ahold of Mr. Webb. He told Webb that Johnny had been trying to get to Birmingham to find his brother who was adopted by some people named Jennison. Since we're the only Jennisons in the phone book, Webb got our number right away from the operator.

"Webb said Johnny wanted to catch another freight, but Linc Fraiser wouldn't let him."

"Thank heavens for that!" Momma said. She smiled at me, and her face just lit up with happiness. She took both my hands. "Looks like you're going to see your brother, sweetie."

"So, Johnny's all right, then?" I wanted to make sure. "I'm sure he is," Daddy said. "Linc Fraiser said he was all right, and Mr. Webb said Fraiser is a good man. Said he trusts him completely. Mr. Webb said he could ask Fraiser to have Johnny at the plantation house tomorrow. Webb said if we could get to Savannah tomorrow, he'll meet us and take us straight to the plantation. What do you think? We'll have to leave today. We'll have to drive to Montgomery. The Atlantic Coast Line has an overnight train that will get us to Savannah in the morning, if I can get us reservations, that is."

"Try!" said Momma. "Let's go!" I said.

Daddy called a friend he had who was with the Atlantic Coast Line. After he knew we had the reservations, Daddy called Mr. Webb back. Four hours later we were in the station wagon on the road to Montgomery. Jackson came with us to bring the car home. At 6:45 we were on the train heading for Savannah.

⌒

That trip to Savannah was the first train trip I didn't enjoy. I was itching to get there and find Johnny. I think Momma and Daddy felt the same way.

That night, I even slept bad, which I don't ever do on a train. Every time the train would stop, I'd wake up thinking we were in Savannah. I must have woke up a dozen times. By the time we rolled into the Union Station in Savannah, I was ready to bust. My folks were on edge, too. I think the suspense and my impatience was about to drive 'em nuts.

Mr. Webb was there waiting for us. He spotted us and came up and introduced himself. He was a tall, nice-looking man with iron-gray hair and a neatly trimmed mustache.

"It's a pleasure to meet you folks," he said. "Let's don't waste any time. If we get goin', we can get to the plantation by noon. Linc and the boy should be waiting for us."

He knew we would have a lot of bags and had brought a station wagon. A few minutes after we got off the train, we were headed for the Webb plantation.

It was a long drive on those Georgia country roads. They were paved, but that's about all you could say for 'em. Still, there wasn't any traffic to speak of, just an old farm truck or Model-T Ford now and then. Nothing to see but pasture and cows and swamp and trees with moss hanging down. Once in a while we'd pass a rickety mule-drawn wagon usually with a poor-looking colored man in overalls driving it.

It was hot and we had all the windows down, but even

with the air blowing in, we were still hot. Finally, we came to a little town called Turpentine and there was the Blackwater river. We turned onto a dirt road and followed the river for about ten miles and came to some big, stone pillars. One of them had a brass plaque on it that said "Belle Ile."

"Welcome to Belle Ile," Mr. Webb said. "It's almost noon. I hope they'll be waiting for us at the house."

Chapter Fifteen

Johnny

ME AND LINC was still light-hearted the day before we went to the plantation house to call Mr. Webb. We lazed around on the dock all morning. Linc was working on his reading, asking me a word now and then. I was laying on the dock with my head on Hooter reading a book I had borrowed from the plantation, *Treasure Island.* It was a humdinger. That afternoon we went fishing and caught some nice bream for supper. After Linc cleaned the fish, we went over to the beach for a swim. We got back to the house feeling fresh and cool for a change.

Linc started supper while I went out on the island to bring in some more firewood. After supper, which was good as usual, we took the dishes down to the dock to let 'em soak and sat down there watching the sunset. We hadn't seen no more of Hepburn, which suited me fine. I wasn't feeling like seeing those hot coal eyes glowing out in that black water.

"Stayin' here with you has been the best time in my life, Linc," I said. "When I was with Aunt Min, I couldn't do nothin' right. She told me every day I wasn't no good, an' I felt like she was right. I don't feel like that no more."

"You a good boy, Johnny," Linc told me, "and smart, too.

"Anybody can teach ol' Linc to read got to be smart, and that ain't all you teach me. Linc done got used to livin' all alone out here. Now I got in mind that bein' alone ain't the bes' way to be. You done got me used to havin' comp'ny. When you not here no mo', Johnny, I believes I gon' make me a change."

"What you goin' to do, Linc?"

"Last time I see Mr. Webb he tol' me he might be wantin' to move back to the plantation. Mr. Webb tol' me he been seein' a nice widow lady in Savannah. He say he was studyin' on gettin' married. Wouldn't surprise me none if he did. His first wife be dead, long time now. If he do git married, he say he fix up the house and yard and all and give me a sho 'nuff job lookin' after the outside stuff. He say he fix up that little house again, an' I could live there. He been talkin' 'bout bringin' Bessie and Joe Carter up from Savannah. Bessie cook fo' Mr. Webb down there, and Joe be the butler. They purty nice folks. If Mr. Webb gits married, and him and his wife was to move to the plantation with Joe and Bessie, I believes I gon' take that job. I'd have me some comp'ny, and I could make some mo' money, too. Save up 'nuff fo' a motor. You know, Johnny, Linc can row all day, but sometimes I gits a little rheumatism and don't feel like it."

"What about this place, Linc?"

"House be right here, honey. I loves the swamp. I be comin' out here when I has time off."

"Linc, I been wondering somethin'." "What's that, honey?"

"I don't know if those folks will want me, but if I do find my brother and go live with him, could both of us come back to see you some time?"

"Sho you can, honey. Hee, hee, hee! Lord, chile! Linc gon' think he seein' double!"

The next morning we went to the plantation house to call Mr. Webb. Linc got him on the phone right off, and I sat there a long time while Linc told him the story. Mr. Webb asked Linc some questions and Linc explained best he could. I heard Linc say:

"…Yas, suh, we be here…... Yas, suh, we goin' to wait right here." He hung up.

"Johnny, Mr. Webb goin' to try to find those folks. He say it might take some time. We got to wait here 'til he call back."

Linc had already figured that we might have to be at the plantation for a while, so we had brung Hooter with us and some supplies. We got our mattresses down cause we were used to sleeping in the front hall. It was goin' to be a whole lot nicer this time 'cause we weren't worried about nothing. That afternoon we got some books and worked on Linc's reading and writing.

It was late the next morning when Mr. Webb called back. He told Linc that he had found the Jennisons and, best of all, that they had been looking for me. He said he thought he could get Mr. and Mrs. Jennison and Will to the plantation house by noon tomorrow. I was goin' to see my brother!

After Linc talked to Mr. Webb, we decided to go on back to the swamp and come back the next day to meet up with the Jennisons. Both of us felt more at home at Linc's place, so we put the mattresses back, got our stuff together and climbed in the boat with Hooter. Linc said his shoulders were acting up some with rheumatism, so I did most of the rowing. My hands were tough by now, and I had got pretty good at it. With all the good food and exercise I'd been getting, I was a whole lot stronger than before. Linc said I didn't look half starved no more. On the way back we stopped at the trotline and, for once, came up empty.

"Look like red beans and rice ag'in, Johnny," Linc said. I didn't mind. The way Linc done 'em, they was always a treat.

We got back to the house and Linc fired up the stove while I put our things away. Linc fixed up a big pot of beans so we'd have enough for another meal. When they were simmering, we went on over to the beach for a swim. We got to the beach, and there was the biggest snapping turtle I ever saw layin' there in the sun. Hooter barked at it and it stuck out its neck about eight inches and hissed at her.

"Hush! Hooter," Linc said, and the turtle slid in the water and swam off.

"That's the first time I heard Hooter bark," I says. "Snappin' turtle the onliest thing Hooter bark at," Linc told me. "She scared of 'em. Hooter purty smart." "She sure is."

"Linc?"

"What, honey?"

"Reckon one of them turtles might ever get ahold of your tallywhacker?"

"Heck, I ain't never studied on that. Shoot! Now that you brung it up, I believes I gon' to float on my back."

"Me, too!" I said.

I fed Hooter while Linc dished up the red beans and rice. The food was good as ever, but Linc didn't eat much.

We had figured on having another writing lesson, but Linc went over and sat on his bunk.

"Honey, Linc don't feel so good this evenin'. I believes I gon' get up on this here bed."

"What's wrong, Linc?"

"Reckon it this rheumatism, Johnny. I feels stiff. Kind of sore. I be all right tomorrow."

"I'll take care of the dishes, Linc," I says. "Then, I'll read you some of this *Treasure Island*. It's prime."

"I'd like that, honey. I sho would."

I got back from the dock and lit the lantern on the kitchen table. I sat at the table with my book and read a chapter out loud, but when I looked up, I seen Linc was asleep. I was some pooped myself, so I went out to pee, got a drink and came in and put out the lantern. I flopped out on my quilts, and Hooter come over next to me and licked my face. The bugs and the frogs were singing loud. I went to sleep with my hand on Hooter, thinking about seeing Will.

I woke up in the pitch dark when I heard Linc moaning and talking. I thought he was having another nightmare. I got the lamp lit and went over to his bed, but I couldn't wake him up. He was shaking and sweating. I put my hand on his head. It was burning up. Linc was sick...out of his head with fever.

I didn't know what to do. He'd get a chill, and I'd cover him up, then he'd get too hot and kick off the quilt. I got a pan with some water and wiped off his head with a cool, wet rag. Then he'd start to shake again.

Long about dawn, the fever broke, and Linc started to make sense again. I gave him a drink of water.

"Johnny, Linc purty sick. This here fever...I done had it befo'. Las' time I be sick three, fo' days. You think you can find yo' way to the plantation in the skiff?"

"I don't know, Linc. Seems like you always go a different way. It's mighty confusin'. I don't think I'd like to try. Anyway, I ain't leavin' you."

"Bes' you don' try. I be better soon. That ol' Mr. Jakes talkin' 'bout me nursemaidin' you. Look like he done got it backwards. You nursemaidin' me."

Linc went to sleep. I ate some cold beans and rice and lay down on a couple of quilts, and I went to sleep, too. When I woke up it was afternoon, and Linc's fever was starting to come back. I knew we wasn't goin' to make it to the plantation house that day.

By late in the afternoon Linc's eyes were bright with fever, and he said he ached something fierce. By the time it was dark, he was as sick as before...maybe worse.

That night went on forever. I'd manage to get a little sleep and then Linc would holler, and I'd get up and wipe his head and try to settle him down. He'd lay there and toss and mutter. Look right at me but not see me. He'd have chills; I'd cover him up, then he'd be burning up. Sometimes he knew who I was, and sometimes he didn't. When his mind was clear, I'd get him water. He'd be really thirsty from sweating so much and from the fever.

That next morning, the fever broke again. I got the stove goin' and cooked us both some fried eggs. Linc ate a little and drank a lot of water. I fed Hooter and went to the outhouse. That afternoon we had a thunderstorm. The sky got real black in the west and the storm came bumbling and grumbling across the swamp. I could see the lightning shooting into the grass flats. It blew hard, and the gusts of wind carried sheets of rain sweeping in over the house. It cooled things off a lot. The coolness made Linc more comfortable. He was better most of the day, but long about evening, he started to shake and the fever hit him again.

That night was like the other nights but not as bad. The fever broke way before dawn and Linc went into a peaceful sleep. When he slept, I did, too, like a dead person.

It was late the next morning when I woke up. Linc was cool but real weak. We was two days late getting to the plantation house to meet up with the Jennisons.

Chapter Sixteen

Will

JOHNNY AND LINC weren't waiting for us. We went right straight through the house and down to the dock. Nobody. We looked up the river. Nobody on the river. We sat down on some benches on the dock and waited and wondered where they were. At one o'clock Mr. Webb said:

"Something's wrong. They should have been here two hours ago. Linc doesn't have a watch but he guesses the time pretty close by the height of the sun. He would have been here by now, if something wasn't wrong.

Momma smacked her fist on the bench.

"Damn!" she said. "I...want...to...find...that...boy!"

"Let me think," Daddy said. "Can you take us to Linc Fraiser's place in your boat, Beau?" Daddy asked Mr. Webb.

"I don't think I could find it," Mr. Webb said. "He took me there once years ago when he first built it. It's really tucked back up in the swamp. I know it's not too far from Lost Lake, but I don't remember which creeks to take. There are so many creeks out there you could wander around for days and not find it. You'd need an airplane to find it." We sat there thinking.

"Uncle Todd!" I said. Daddy looked at me. His eyebrows went up.

"Is there a place around here you could land a light airplane?" Daddy asked Mr. Webb.

"Sure, the big field out back behind the hay barn. Lease it to my neighbor. He runs some cattle on it, and they keep the grass down pretty good. I'm sure you could land a plane there."

"Let's go look at it," Daddy said, standing up. "Can we use the phone?"

"Help yourself," said Mr. Webb.

"Allie's brother has a Steerman biplane. He's a top-notch pilot. Allie, while we go look at the field, run up to the house and get on the phone and see if you can track down Todd."

When we got back from the field, Momma was pacing up and down by the phone.

"The newspaper is trying to find him," she said. The phone jangled and we all jumped. It was Todd, and Momma told him where we were and gave him an idea of what was goin' on. Then she listened.

"...You've got a deadline for the paper? Dammit, Todd, what do I care about your deadline! We've got a missing child down here.

"...I will not calm down! Are you going to help us or not?"

She listened, breathing hard through her nose and staring at the wall.

"He wants you," she said, handing the phone to Mr. Webb.

"Todd, this is Beau Webb. I own the plantation here. Linc Fraiser works for me as a caretaker. He's the one who found the boy.

"...That's right. Linc has a little house way up in the swamp. We're pretty sure that's where the boy is.

"...No, Linc was supposed to meet us here today. We don't know why they didn't show up. Something's wrong.

"...Yes, I believe we can find the place from the air. I know where to start looking.

"...Landing here shouldn't be a problem. We've just been to check out a field where you can land. Frank and I agree that it looks fine. There aren't any cattle there now, so you don't have to worry about that.

"...Sure, here's what you do: About a hundred miles northwest of Savannah up Route 42, there's a little town called Turpentine. You can find it on your maps. It's on the Blackwater river. Fly straight to Turpentine and pick up the Blackwater river. Turn southeast and follow the river for about ten miles...."

Around three thirty, Mr. Webb took me with him to Turpentine to pick up groceries. We got back about five and, soon after that, Momma was putting together a supper of cold cuts and salad when we heard Uncle Todd's plane come over. We all ran out of the house and climbed in the station wagon. We got to the big pasture just as Uncle Todd's plane rolled to a stop near the barn. We ran over to greet him.

"Well, well," Momma said, giving him a hug, "look who dropped in! Just in time for dinner." Uncle Todd knew Momma wasn't much of a cook and couldn't resist teasing her.

"You cooking, Allie?" He asked, grinning. "What's for supper...cold cuts?"

"How'd you guess, big brother!" Momma grinned back at him and punched him on the shoulder.

Uncle Todd met Mr. Webb and they started right in planning how to search for Johnny and Linc Fraiser. Luckily Mr. Webb had a supply of gas that he kept for his boat and his tractor, and they were able to gas up the plane. By the time the plane was ready, and we had eaten supper, it was too late to start searching. We would have to start in the morning.

"Oh brother," I said, "more waiting!"

The next morning we had an early breakfast and all went out to the plane. We had figured out that I was the only one Johnny would recognize, and I wanted to go anyway. I loved flying with Uncle Todd. He and Mr. Webb were planning what to do.

"Todd, Lost Lake lies almost due east of the house. I think if we fly over the lake and then fly a pattern of circles behind the lake, we ought to find the house. The dock will be easier to see than the house 'cause Linc's house is built back in the trees."

"I'll fly up to one end of the lake and then work my way back towards the other end," Todd told him. "That OK?"

"Sounds good," he said. "Let's get goin'."

The Steerman had twin cockpits, and I sat in the back with Mr. Webb. He had a board with a sheet of paper taped to it so he could make a map of the creeks that led to Linc Fraiser's house. Mr. Webb had told us that he had used an airplane to check out his timber holdings and that he was used to figuring out things from the air.

Daddy pulled the propeller for Uncle Todd. The plane had a Lycoming rotary engine, and it caught on the first pull.

Uncle Todd revved it up and we rolled down to the end of the field and turned around.

"Here we go!" Uncle Todd yelled and gave it full throttle. We went bouncing down the field zigzagging to avoid the rough spots. We were up! Headed out over the swamp. I looked down and waved at Momma and Daddy.

We circled for a long time out past the south end of the lake and didn't see anything. Uncle Todd looked back at Mr. Webb and raised his eyebrows.

"Farther out," Mr. Webb yelled into the wind, "more circles!"

There was so much swamp out there. I looked and looked, and we circled. After another hour we had flown over thousands of acres of swamp with no sign of a house. Uncle Todd shouted back at us that we needed to go back and gas up, and he banked the plane into a turn and headed back to the plantation house. After we got back and gassed up and ate some sandwiches, it was pushing three o'clock. I was ready to go up again, but Uncle Todd pointed out over the swamp. A huge thunderstorm was building out there with great black clouds piling up on each other.

"We can't fly into that," he said, taking some rope and metal stakes out of the plane. "We've got to tie the plane down. A storm like that could flip it over in a second."

By the time the storm had moved through, it was too late to go back up. We were a mighty glum bunch sitting around that night, munching cold cuts.

"I think we'll find 'em tomorrow," Mr. Webb said. "I believe we've been looking too far to the south. We'll try the north end of the lake tomorrow."

"I sure hope we find them soon," Momma said. "I'm worried sick."

The next morning we had been flying circles for about an hour, and I was starting to get discouraged again. Mr. Webb motioned for Uncle Todd to head farther out over the swamp. I rubbed my eyes which were sore from the wind. When I looked again, I saw something!

Off to the left there was a thin line of smoke rising out of some trees on what looked like an island. I touched Uncle Todd's shoulder and pointed to it. He banked the plane and we headed down to get a better look. As we flew over the island, a dock came into view, sticking out into a creek. Then I could see a little house under the trees. I didn't see anybody, but smoke was coming out of a stove pipe on the back side of the

house. Uncle Todd held the plane in a tight circle and we came around again. As we were coming around, a boy ran down on the dock. He had red hair. I stood up as tall as I dared in the cockpit. Mr. Webb had his arms around my waist. I waved and screamed into the wind.

"Johnny!"

He waved and cupped his hands around his mouth. With the engine noise and the wind, I couldn't have heard him...but I did.

"Will!"

Chapter Seventeen

Johnny

AFTER I SEEN Will, I went runnin' back to the house.

"It's Will, Linc! It's Will! In a airplane! I seen him! We waved at each other!

"I heard it, honey. I reckon Mr. Webb done forgit how to find Linc's house."

"There was three of 'em in the plane, Linc, the pilot and one man in back with Will."

"You see what the one in back look like, Johnny?" "Seems like he had gray hair. Maybe a mustache." "That Mr. Webb. He be comin' back in a boat soon. Johnny, you got to help Linc get clean up. I don' smell so good."

I had already helped Linc to the outhouse and back. He was so weak he couldn't walk without me, but the fever was gone. I finished cooking breakfast. We ate and then I took a pan to the river and dipped up some water. I brought it back to the house and soaped-up a cloth and helped Linc to wash. I got another pan of water so we could get the soap off, and then Linc pulled on some clean clothes. I took his clothes and mine over to the beach. We had taken a washtub over there.

I washed up the clothes and rinsed them in the river and spread 'em out on the porch to dry. When I got back to the house. Linc said:

"Johnny, you take a kitchen chair out on the porch and help ol' Linc git out there so's he can see the dock. I wouldn't miss you an' yo' brother gettin' back together fo' a thousand dollars, and Linc ain't never had that much!"

"You sure had me scared, Linc. I thought you was goin' to die."

"If you hadn't tuk care of me, Johnny, I be dead fo' sho. You give me water and keep me cool down. I sho thank you, honey."

"My goodness, Linc, you saved my life before I even met you when you shot that snake. Seems like to me we're even."

I put a kitchen chair out on the porch for Linc and helped him to it. Then I went down on the dock and looked up the creek. Hooter come over and put her nose in my hand. After a time, she started to whine.

"They's comin'!" Linc said. "Won't be long now."

Sure enough, after a few minutes, I seen a boat coming up the creek. Will was in it with two men and a lady with red hair. They was waving. I raised my hand to wave back, but it seemed like I couldn't move.

"Lord, Lord!" said Linc.

The boat bumped the dock and Will jumped out. We just stood there looking at each other in amazement. Will reached out and put his left hand on my shoulder, and I done the same to him.

"Hey, Johnny...," he says.

"Hey, Will...," I says.

Then we was hugging each other, and all the grown-ups started to cheer.

Then Will took me over and introduced me to his momma and daddy. His daddy took my hand and said:

"Johnny, we are so glad to see you. We've been tryin' hard to find you."

The red-headed lady was Will's momma. She got on one knee and put her hands on my shoulders. She pulled me to her and put her arms around me. I ain't never had such a hug. Tears were drippin' down on my neck, and, to tell the truth, I was a little leaky myself.

She smiled at me and reached out for Will and hugged us both for a long time. She smelled like honeysuckle.

When she turned me loose, I took Will by the arm and led him up to the house to meet Linc. Will's momma and daddy and Mr. Webb come, too.

"This is Linc," I says, "my best friend, and this is Hooter." Linc said he was mighty glad to meet Will and shook his hand.

"Lord, Johnny!" Linc said. "When you gits yo' hair cut, nobody gon' to know who is who!"

Mr. Webb said, "Linc, you look terrible. What happened to you?"

"I been purty sick, Mr. Webb. Got the fever. Johnny look after me. I sho is sorry I couldn't git us back to the house when I say I would."

"We knew something was wrong," Mr. Webb told him. "I'm glad you're better, Linc."

"Yas, suh, Linc all right now but mos'ly too weak to walk. I be dead if Johnny hadn't tuk care of me." Everybody looked at me.

"'Course I did," I said. "Linc's been lookin' after me for a month. First thing he done was keep me from gettin' snake bit." I told 'em about Linc shooting the snake after I got off of the boxcar. Mr. Jennison come over and shook hands with Linc.

"My wife and I will never forget the way you looked after Johnny," he said, holding on to Linc's hand and looking right in his eyes. "Never."

Mrs. Jennison come over and took his other hand. "Thank you, Linc," she said smilin' at him. Linc looked up at 'em.

"You folks don' need to thank Linc. This here boy sat up with me when that fever had me bad. Me and Johnny tuk care of each other. Like he say, we friends."

Before we left, I took the Jennisons and Will up to Linc's house to show it to them. They said it was a fine little place, which it is…fine as anybody could ever want. While they were getting Linc in the boat, Johnny and me run up the path so's I could show him the swimming beach.

We all piled into the boat and, with all of us and Hooter and the pig food, it was plenty full and sat pretty low in the water, but the motor putted us right along. We got to the plantation house quicker than we would have if we'd been rowing.

As we come in sight of the dock, I could see a tall man standing there waving.

"That's my Uncle Todd," Will said. "He was flying the airplane." When we got to the dock, Will introduced me to his uncle, who just stood there shaking his head and grinning.

"Amazing!" he said, "It's just amazing!"

⌒

Mr. Webb and Mr. Jennison carried Linc up to the house.

He said he'd like to stretch out on the porch swing, so they got him comfortable there with a couple of cushions. While they were getting him settled, we heard the airplane taking off. Will's uncle was in a big hurry to get back to Birmingham. He held the plane in a tight, low turn, circling the plantation house...waving to us. Then the plane climbed and headed towards Birmingham.

⌒

"Linc, I'm goin' to call Dr. Klein over in Tomkins and get him to come over and take a look at you."

"Yas, suh," Linc said. "I 'preciate it, Mr. Webb." I went over to Linc and put my hand on his shoulder. I had gotten used to me and Linc being together.

"What about this boy here?" Linc asked.

There were some iron chairs and some rocking chairs on that porch, and Mr. Jennison pulled 'em around. Everybody sat down. I sat on the floor by Linc.

"We need to explain some stuff," Mr. Jennison said.

He told me and Linc how hard they had been trying to

find me. He said that when our folks were killed, him and
Mrs. Jennison had tried to get me and Will both, but Aunt
Min had wanted to keep me. Then he told us about goin' to
the house and meeting Aunt Min and said that he thought
she was crazy.

"We don't want you to go back to that lady, son. We want
to adopt you."

"You mean you'd be like my momma and daddy, and I
would live with youall and Will?"

"Not 'like' your momma and daddy, Johnny," Mrs. Jennison
said. "We'd be your momma and daddy, your legal parents."

"You mean you want me for good?" I asked.

"You bet we do!" she said. "We love Will and have lots of
fun with him. If we had you, too, there'd be twice as many
boys to love and twice as much fun. In fact, with the two
of you working together, I bet it would be four times as
much fun!"

"I sure would like that," I told em. "Except for bein'
with Linc, I ain't never had no home." Linc was grinning
'cause what he'd said about the Jennisons was turning out
to be true.

"Here's the bad part, Johnny," Mr. Jennison said. "We have
to go back to Columbia, Tennessee, and have a court hearing
to try to get custody of you, so that you can legally be our boy.
We're not sure the judge will go along with what we want.
What we're afraid of is that your aunt might try to keep custody out of pure meanness. She has legally adopted you, and
she's your blood kin. That puts her in a pretty strong posi-
tion. A judge might believe her and not us. Still, we've got
no choice. We've got to do this legally. If we just took you, we
could be charged with kidnapping."

"Mr. Jennison, I understand what you're gettin' at, but if a judge made me go back to Aunt Min, I would run off again." Mr. And Mrs. Jennison looked at each other. Finally, Mr. Jennison says:

"The only thing I can tell you right now, Johnny, is that we have to take this one step at a time. If we can convince a judge that your aunt is crazy, maybe he will take our side. Right now, I want Allie to call her dad, who is a judge in Birmingham, and let him advise us how to go about all this."

Mrs. Jennison went to telephone, and I climbed up on the swing with Linc. We could hear her in the house talking on the phone.

"How you feeling, Linc?" I asked him.

"Linc feelin' fine, honey. Jes' weak. I be fine now." Mrs. Jennison came back.

"Judge is goin' to call an attorney he knows in Columbia to help us get a quick hearing," she told us. "We don't want Johnny to have to go back to the Brashers while we wait for a hearing."

"Look," said Mr. Webb. "Here's what we'll do: You folks take the station wagon right now and head for Columbia. I'll stay here with Linc until he gets his strength back. Later on, I'll catch the train from Savannah to Montgomery. Frank, if you could drive down from Birmingham and meet me, I could stay with youall for a couple of days and then drive the station wagon back to Savannah. I haven't been to Birmingham for years. This will give me a good excuse for a visit."

"But you'd be stuck here," Mr. Jennison said.

"So what," Mr. Webb said. "I was born and raised here. I know everybody for miles around. I have a phone. Jonah Hadley, at the grocery store in Turpentine, will be glad to bring out whatever I need. If I really want to go to town, I have the boat."

"How you goin' to get from here back to Savannah?" Mr. Jennison asked him.

"When Linc's on his feet, Joe, my butler, can drive up here in my Buick and take me back. A little quiet time before the wedding is just what I need…some reading…some fishing…I'm starting to relax just thinking about it."

"Wedding?" Mrs. Jennison asked him.

"I'm getting married next month. A lovely widow lady. Grace Fellows is her name. She moved to Savannah from Atlanta last year. I'll telephone Grace after youall leave. She's so busy getting ready for the wedding, she'll be glad to get rid of me for a while."

The Jennisons jumped up to congratulate him. Linc was right about Mr. Webb getting married.

"I just don't like leaving you here without a car, Beau," Mr. Jennison said.

"Listen, Frank," Mr. Webb said, "the important thing is for you to get this boy into your family. I wouldn't feel right if I didn't do everything in my power to help you with that." Mrs. Jennison went over and hugged Mr. Webb and kissed him on the cheek.

"OK, Beau," Mr. Jennison said. "We'll take you up on the car on one condition."

"What is it?" Mr. Webb asked.

"The train ticket to Montgomery is on me."

"Done!" said Mr. Webb. "Now, you folks get started." "Before we leave, Beau," Mr. Jennison said, "I need to make a couple of more phone calls, if I may. I want to call Sheriff Pratt in Columbia and the chief of police in Birmingham to let them know we've found Johnny. Right now, the police still have him listed as a missing person. I'll get Sheriff Pratt to notify the Brashers. I want him to tell them that we want custody and that we are goin' to try for a quick hearing. That will give them more time to get their own attorney lined up if they want to try to keep Johnny." Mr. Jennison must have seen me look funny, 'cause he put his hand on my shoulder.

"It's got to be done, Johnny," he told me. "We've got to do everything right. I don't want your aunt saying we didn't bother to inform her that we found you."

Fifteen minutes later, we loaded up the station wagon, and all of us said goodbye to Mr. Webb. I shook his hand and hugged Hooter. It was hard to say goodbye to Linc. It was all I could do not to cry.

"I'm goin' to come back and see you, Linc," I told him. "I promise."

"I know you be comin' back, honey. Be sho an' bring Will. Don't you never forget that Linc loves you."

"I love you, too, Linc," I said givin' him a hug. We all climbed in the station wagon. I was on my way back to Tennessee.

Chapter Eighteen

Will

*T*HAT TRIP IN THE CAR to Columbia was strange. We had Johnny, but we didn't know if we'd be able to keep him. It was so hot we had to roll all the windows down, and the wind noise made it hard to talk. Momma had seen Johnny was tired and had borrowed a pillow from Mr. Webb. The back of the station wagon was full of bags, so I rode in front in the middle, and Momma told Johnny to stretch out on the back seat. He was asleep before we had gone five miles.

The roads were bad and we bumped along in the heat. We played word games for a while, twenty questions and ghost, but, after a time, we got tired of talking against the wind and quit. I'd see a white horse or mule and lick my thumb. You had to put your wet thumb on your palm and then smack the spit with your fist. It was something you were supposed to do for luck. I stuck my two pointer fingers in my mouth and bit down on the backs of my fingernails then hooked the two fingers together and pulled to see if it hurt. It did.

It seemed like forever bumping along those back roads at forty miles an hour. The scenery sure wasn't much to look at, poor-looking farm houses, falling down barns, washed out red-clay fields with burnt-up, scraggly corn that wasn't worth picking....Finally, we crossed the Tennessee border and Daddy stopped for gas at a little country gas station with a blue-and-white "Pure" sign out front. Johnny woke up when the car stopped and we all climbed out. It was hard for Johnny and me to quit looking at each other. It was so much like looking in the mirror. He was a little more sunburned than me, but he was clean and wasn't skinny like when I first saw him. He hadn't had a haircut in a long while, so his hair was longer than mine, but except for that and the sunburn, I couldn't see any difference. I guess we must have been real close for that first two years, though, because having Johnny back was starting to feel real normal to me.

We went out back to the men's room and it turned out to be an outhouse with a crescent moon cut in the door and "His" painted over it. I went in first. When I came out, I wrinkled my nose and rolled my eyes up.

"Pee-yew!" I said, and he started to giggle as he went in.

"Pee-yew, is right!" He said. "Ugh!" We were still giggling when we got back to the car.

"What you boys giggling about?" Momma asked us. "Stinky outhouse," I said.

"Mine was, too," she said and made a face, and we all started to giggle all over again.

Daddy came back from paying for the gas with four cold bottles of Co'Cola and some peanut butter crackers and put them on the hood.

"Where's the men's room?" he said. We all pointed out back and started to laugh even harder. Daddy looked puzzled. "Did I say something funny?"

"Men's room…" Momma said, holding her sides, and we laughed some more.

Johnny and me swapped off. He got in the front, and we started off again. We saw a white mule, and Momma licked her thumb and stamped her palm. Johnny asked her what it meant, and she said it was for good luck and took his hand to show him how to do it.

"Lord have mercy, honey, look at your hands! What in the world have you been doing?"

"Me and Linc had to do a lot of rowin'," Johnny told her. "I was gettin' pretty good at it."

"You and Linc must have had quite a time," Momma said. "I hope you'll tell us all about it when we don't have to talk above all this noise."

"Yes'm, I will," he said. "There's a lots I want to tell you. A whole lots."

Well 'course that made us mighty curious, but we kept quiet. We didn't want to push him.

We pulled into Columbia about supper time. We didn't have any trouble getting two rooms in the Bethel Hotel. We were hot and tired. Johnny had never stayed in a hotel before and, while Daddy was checking us in, he was looking around, wide-eyed.

"We went up to our rooms which were connecting, and Momma came in and ran us a bath. She left some of my clothes on the bed for Johnny. Without even thinking about it, me and Johnny shucked off our clothes and both climbed into the tub at the same time. I stuck my fist in the water, pointed the opening at Johnny and squeezed a handful of water, which squirted Johnny in the nose. He sat there looking amazed with water dripping off of his nose.

"How'd you do that?" He wanted to know. I showed him and he squirted me. Pretty quick, we had a squirting match goin' on…both of us squirting with both hands. Momma heard us splashing and laughing and came in.

"Hey, you guys! Stop. You're getting the joint wet." I saw Johnny look scared for a second.

"We'll mop it up, Momma," I told her.

"Wash your faces and back of your ears real good," she said and left.

"She's not mad?" Johnny asked.

"Naw. Momma gets mad at Daddy but not much at me," I told him. After we got dressed, we went into Momma and Daddy's room. Daddy was just getting off the phone from talking to Judge in Birmingham.

"Judge really came through for us," he said. "The lawyer he called, Aaron Steiner, arranged for a preliminary hearing tomorrow, so we can have temporary custody of Johnny. It's goin' to be at one thirty in the afternoon. At ten in the morning, we have a meeting with Steiner, who is goin' to be our lawyer. Judge says that Mr. Steiner is a good lawyer and is well-liked by the judges in Columbia. The Brashers have been notified about Johnny and about us wanting custody. They don't appear to object to having a quick hearing. It might be possible to get a custody hearing as early as Thursday."

"What day is today?" Johnny asked. "In the swamp, days don't mean nothing. Me and Linc never knew what day it was."

"Today's Monday," Daddy told him. "In a few days, we might have this all behind us."

"I sure hope it comes out the right way," Johnny said.

Later on, when we were in the dinning room waiting for dinner, Johnny reached for his water and knocked over the pepper shaker. He looked up at Momma real quick, and I saw that same scared look in his eyes. Momma put her hand on his hand and she said:

"Johnny, I want to tell you something about our family. You're not ours yet, but if you do join our family, I want you to know what to expect. Mr. Jennison and I won't ever punish you for mistakes. Not ever. Mistakes are the way people learn. If you or Will break something or spill something, if it was by accident, you won't ever be punished for it. Now let me tell you about punishment: We don't do any leg-switching in this family or any goin'-to-bed-without-supper. If you boys drive me nuts, which boys are good at doing, you might get a swat on your rear end. If you do something you've been told not to do, you might have to spend some time in your room. The worst punishment you would get would be losing something fun like goin' to a movie or having a friend over. The time Will set the woods on fire, we sent his best friend Butch home and Will had a mighty boring weekend."

"What if I was to spill this milk right here?" Johnny asked.

"We'd mop it up," Momma said.

"No whippin'?"

"No whipping. Not ever. Right, Will?"

"Right," I told him. "If I was goin' to get any whippin's, I sure would have got 'em by now."

Johnny was shaking his head with amazement.

"No whippin's..." he said. "That would be wonderful!" That night after dinner Momma took us up to the room.

She knew Johnny was still tired, and she said she wanted us in bed early. She said we could stay up and read or talk but had to get in the bed early. Momma had brought extra clothes for Johnny. After we were in our pajamas, we both climbed up in the big double bed, and Momma came in to tell us good-night. She and Daddy were goin' to sit on the hotel porch and talk for a while. She hugged me and gave me a kiss and then did the same to Johnny. After she left, Johnny said:

"I always wondered what it would be like to get a hug and a kiss at bedtime. I used to try to get a picture of our real Momma doin' that, but it weren't no good 'cause I couldn't remember her face."

Then he told me about looking out of the freight car and seeing a woman hugging a little girl and how it made him so sad. We lay in that big bed and talked and talked. I told him about my life in Birmingham; about our home, about Jenny May and Jackson and about Butch and Charlie and some of my other friends. I told him about the school I went to in Mountain Brook. Johnny told me about his life with his aunt and uncle. It was awful. He didn't have any good friends because his aunt made him come home right after school to do chores. He never got to go home with school friends or have them over. The only time he got to play was at recess. Just like me, he liked to read but his aunt wouldn't get him any books. She said they were sinful. She whipped him for every little mistake and sent him to bed with no supper. He said that he really might have starved if it hadn't been for Sarah. The more I heard, the sadder I got.

"I hate to hear about that, Johnny," I told him. "I've been living in a nice home with a Momma and Daddy and plenty to eat while you been stuck with almost nothing. It isn't fair."

"I don't reckon it has to be fair," he said. "I did have a wonderful time with Linc."

I asked him about what happened in the swamp with Linc, and boy was I surprised. Johnny hadn't had any life at all with the Brashers, but in that time with Linc, he'd had more adventures than most boys ever get. The story about the alligator getting Bobby Scagg gave me goose bumps.

We lay there in the dark for a while with only a pale shine from the street lights coming up through the oak trees.

"Will?" "What?"

"When my room was this dark at my aunt's place, I used to get scared, but when I was in the middle of that swamp with Linc in the pitch dark with all them jungley noises outside, I didn't never get scared. I ain't scared with you here neither."

"Me neither," I said.

"I reckon bein' scared has somethin' to do with bein' lonesome," he said. "If there's somebody around who loves you, you don't hardly get scared."

I reached over and put my hand on his shoulder and he did the same to me. I didn't tell him I was glad to have him back, and he didn't tell me. We knew.

Chapter Nineteen

Johnny

I WAS FEELING like I was in a dream. I was back with Will and with his wonderful parents. He was my brother, but his momma and daddy wasn't my momma and daddy. It was like a pane of glass was between me and Mr. and Mrs. Jennison. It was as hard a time of waiting as I ever hope to have, even worse than when me and Linc was waiting for Bobby Scagg.

That Tuesday morning we went to the lawyer's office and found out some stuff that didn't sound too good. He told us that the judge we were goin' to see was called Judge King. Said he was a narrow-minded man who had lived most of his life in Columbia and didn't think much of big city folks or colored folks. That was bad 'cause the Jennisons were from Birmingham and Sarah Davis was goin' to be the main one telling how Aunt Min treated me. I had never know'd any grown folks besides Sarah except for my teacher, Miss Brownlee. Mr. Steiner, the lawyer, said he would try to get her to come to the hearing. I could have told the judge about Aunt Min, but Mr. Steiner said that a child my age wouldn't be allowed to say nothing at the hearing. That seemed funny to me seeing as I was the one the hearing was about.

Mr. Steiner took us to the Columbia diner for lunch where we all had hamburgers and french fried potatoes. I didn't have no appetite, but the hamburgers was good, and I ate most of mine. After we had lunch, we all set on the benches in the square across from the courthouse and waited 'til it was time to see the judge.

"I hate waiting," I told Mrs. Jennison.

"Me, too, honey," she said. Mr. Jennison looked at his watch.

"It's one twenty-five," he said. "Let's go."

We went on into the courthouse and found the judge's office. There was a waiting room with wooden chairs padded with red leather. A skinny old lady with glasses perched on the end of her nose was settin' there behind a desk. She looked at us when we come in like she had tasted something bad. Daddy told her we were the Jennisons. She said the judge would see us in a few minutes and that we was to set down. After about five minutes, she got up and went into the judge's office and then come back and told us the judge was ready and we was to go on in.

Judge King was a fat, red-faced man with blond, curly hair. I didn't like the look of him, but he give us one big surprise. He told us that Aunt Min was not goin' to try to keep me. I couldn't believe it. All that worry for nothing. The judge said:

"I don't know what the big rush from you folks was. Mrs. Brasher's attorney, Mr. Slade, called me yesterday to say that Mrs. Brasher is not interested in retaining custody of the child. Seems like somebody could have found that out before rushing me up so much. 'Course, under the law, I still

have to determine in a court hearing what's in the child's best interest, but since nobody is contesting what you want, I'm durned if I'm goin' to hurry. My calendar is full up next month. I'm setting the hearing for October tenth." Daddy thanked him and we left. I walked out of the courthouse feeling confused.

"Well, that's a happy surprise," Momma said, "too good to be true."

"Sure is," said Daddy. "I don't know what to make of it." "Looks to me like you're home free," Mr. Steiner said. "I guess I'll see you folks in October at the hearing. It should just be a formality." We all thanked him and headed back to the hotel.

It was too late to drive all the way to Birmingham so Daddy said we'd spend one more night in the hotel. Later that afternoon, Mr. Jennison took me and Will to the barber shop and got us haircuts. I had never been in a barbershop before, 'cause Aunt Min had always cut my hair. I found it mighty interesting. When he finished, the barber put some Bay Rum on our necks and we come out of there real fragrant. After the haircuts, we looked even more alike, and the Jennisons was starting to get us mixed up. Will thought it was funny, but I didn't feel like laughing. I should have been happy, but I weren't. My chest was feeling too full...like something had to come out.

Chapter Twenty

Will

WHEN WE GOT BACK to the hotel after seeing the judge, we all went up to the rooms. Momma and Daddy were talking about what had happened. I saw something was the matter with Johnny. He was staring off into space, and his mouth was pulled down at the corners. He had told me that he used to cry himself to sleep at night when he went to live with the Brashers but that he'd quit when he was four. The only time he'd really cried since then was when he saw that lady kiss her little girl goodnight. I went over and put my hand on his knee. He wouldn't look at me. Momma came over. She sat on the bed by him and put her arm around his shoulder.

"What's wrong, honey?" she said. Johnny bent over and put his face in his hands and started to sob. Momma didn't say anything. She just stroked the back of his head and shooed me and Daddy out of the room. As I left, I looked back and saw her sit Johnny up and fold her arms around him. Daddy and I went on down to the lobby and sat down under a big ceiling fan.

"Johnny's only cried one time since he was little," I said. Daddy put his hand over mine.

"He's got some catching up to do," Daddy said.

"Daddy, is Johnny really ours now...to keep?"

"I believe so, son. We'll have to come back up here for the hearing, but Mr. Steiner said it will just be a formality."

"I can't believe it," I told him.

"Me either," Daddy said. "It was so easy. It's goin' to take some getting used to."

I looked up and saw Momma and Johnny coming into the lobby. They sat down with us.

"Johnny's afraid youall will think he's a crybaby," Momma said.

"Not me," Daddy said. "Me neither," I told him.

"Son," Daddy said to him, "far as I'm concerned, two cries while you're growing up aren't nearly enough." Johnny gave us a quick smile.

"How about an early dinner and a movie?" Daddy asked. "I saw the marquis on the theater when we drove into town. There's a western on."

"I ain't never been to a movie," Johnny said. "Well, then, it's time you went," Momma said. "They're fun!" I told him. "Westerns are great!"

"I just can't believe I ain't never goin' back to Aunt Min, Mr. Jennison," Johnny said.

"Why don't you start calling us Momma and Daddy," Daddy said, putting his hand over Johnny's. "That might help you feel like you're really goin' to stay with us."

"Uh...Daddy," Johnny said, raising his eyebrows. "That's a boy!" Daddy told him. "You'll get used to it."

We all had some more of that country-fried steak that seemed to be the only thing the Bethel hotel liked to serve. I didn't too much care, though. My appetite was picking up after all the worry, and the food tasted pretty good. Johnny did a better job of eating, too.

"Not the Savoy Plaza, is it, Allie?" Daddy grinned at Momma. (When Momma and Daddy went to New York they stayed in a fancy hotel called the Savoy Plaza.)

"Yeah," Momma said, "turnip greens and corn pones just don't show up on the menu at the Savoy Plaza. Wonder why that is?"

"Bunch of Yankees up there!" Daddy said, chuckling.

After dinner we walked to the movie theater. We went on in and got some popcorn. The movie was a western called *Sagebrush Bandits*. It was cowboys blazing away with six shooters and falling off horses and fighting. It wasn't a real good movie, but Johnny was amazed by it. Daddy slept through the whole thing.

The next day we piled into Mr. Webb's station wagon and headed for Birmingham. We had found Johnny and we were goin' home. The thing was, though, it was our home, not Johnny's. We still had to get Johnny to feel like he was one of us.

On the drive from Columbia to Birmingham I cooked up a trick to play on Jenny May.

"Here's what we'll do," I told him. "I got a way we can fool Jenny May..." Johnny listened carefully, and we practiced for a while.

Finally, we pulled up to the house and all piled out of the car. Sure enough, Jenny May was the first person we saw. She came out the front door and when she saw us her mouth dropped open. She stood there looking at me and then Johnny...back and forth, trying to figure out who was who.

"Lord have mercy!" she said. "If that don't beat all!" "I'm Johnny," we both said. Then we pointed at each other and both said: "He's Will."

"Lord!" she said and sat down on the front steps starting to laugh. "Two of you little rascals to run Jenny May 'round. My, my, my!"

Jackson came out to help unload the car, and I introduced him to Johnny.

"Jackson, this is my brother, Johnny," I said.

"Hey, Jackson," Johnny said shaking hands, "nice to meet you."

"Nice to meet you, too," Jackson said. "Things goin' to get confusin' 'round here," he said, chuckling.

Charlie was sure confused. He didn't know who to go to. We both called him, and he sat down, turning his head real fast from me to Johnny and back.

"Looks like he's watching a tennis match," Daddy said. Charlie came over and sniffed me and then he sniffed Johnny. We must have smelled the same, 'cause he still didn't know.

Finally, Charlie just blew a fuse. He lay down between us, put his head on the floor between his paws and started to whine. We both went over to him and loved him up. It didn't take long for Charlie to get the idea that two boys patting him and playing with him was better than one.

I showed Johnny around the house...showed him our bedroom and the daybeds on the porch where we would sleep 'til it got cold. I took him out to the kitchen and showed him the wood-burning stove that Jenny May cooked on, and, then, we went through the little back screen porch where the ice-box was. We went on outside, and I showed him the showers. Then we walked around the back of the house to the pavilion.

"This is my favorite place," I told him. "We eat out here a lot. It's a great place to watch a thunderstorm. I love storms."

"Me, too," said Johnny. "We had some beauties in the swamp."

While we were out on the pavilion, Jenny May brought out some sandwiches and ice tea. All of us sat around the picnic table and ate. Johnny looked a little dazed, and I guess it was a whole lot for him to take in.

After lunch, Daddy went to the office for the afternoon. Said he had a bunch of stuff to catch up on. Momma got busy unpacking.

I took Johnny around some more and showed him all my secret places...how to crawl around the house behind the bushes without being seen, my secret room in the attic under the eaves, the huge boulder in the woods that had a place under it that was almost like a cave.

By the middle of the afternoon we were both tired. I guess the drive down from Columbia, the worry we had been goin' through, and the excitement of getting home had worn us down. We took a stack of comic books on the porch and just lay around on the daybeds, reading.

That night we all had an early supper on the pavilion, and, after sitting around in the twilight for a while, Momma said she wanted us in bed. She must have seen that we were drooping. We took a quick bath and both got into some of my pajamas and went into the library where Momma and Daddy were listening to Jack Benny on the radio. We told 'em goodnight and Momma came out on the screen porch and kissed us goodnight after we were in bed.

I could see it was goin' to be fun sleeping on the porch with Johnny. The daybeds were close together, and we lay there talking...listening to Momma and Daddy laughing at the radio show and the bugs chirrin' outside in the soft summer night. Johnny said sleeping on the screen porch reminded him of goin' to sleep in Linc's little house but not so jungley-sounding. I asked Johnny if he was goin' to tell Momma and Daddy about what happened to him up in the swamp with Linc. He said he was, but that nobody but them and us could know about it. He said Linc had told him that Bobby Scagg's relatives would make bad trouble if they ever found out what had happened. We lay there for a while, not talking, just listening to the nighttime sounds. Johnny must have been thinking the same thing I was, 'cause after a while he said:

"Will...?"

"Yeah...?"

"Do you remember our first daddy?"

"I don't," I told him. "I remember somebody being around, but I don't remember what he looked like. Sometimes I can't even get a good picture of what our first momma looked like."

"Me neither," Johnny said. "I know her hair was gold-colored. Sometimes, I can see her when I dream, but I can't hardly remember her face when I'm awake."

"I see her in a dream, too," I told him. "I'm on a picnic with her. It's confusing 'cause you're in the dream, too. Back before I knew about you, I used to think I was looking at myself in the dream, but it was you."

"Yeah," Johnny said, "I have a dream like that. A picnic. You reckon that could have been one of the last times we was with her?"

"I bet you're right," I said. "I bet you we went on a picnic with her right before they got killed." We lay there thinking...trying to remember.

"Will...?"

"Yeah...?"

"I wish I could remember what they looked like..." "Me, too..."

A few days after we got back, Daddy came home early from the office. We went out to meet him.

"I've got some news about Linc," he said while we were going into the library.

"I talked to Mr. Webb today, Johnny. He's coming in from Savannah on Friday to pick up his station wagon. He'll stay with us a couple of nights. Mr. Webb told me Linc is fine. He's back at his place in the swamp. He's going to stay there 'til Mr. Webb gets the little house fixed up. He told Mr. Webb he sure does miss you. Said he's spending a lot of time talking to Hooter." Johnny lit up when he heard about Linc.

That night we had a family party. A picnic supper on the pavilion. Judge and Sophie and all the Hightowers came over. We met them at the front door. Everybody was amazed to see Johnny and me together. Janie shook hands with Johnny.

"Oh, no," said Henry, "two of 'em!"

"Well, well…here's Plain Jane," I said. Janie, who was pretty in spite of being a tomboy, balled up her right fist.

"You better look out, Will," she said. "I'll bust you."

When Sophie met Johnny she hugged him and planted a big, wet kiss on his cheek. I had warned Johnny that the family was big on kissing. He just wiped off his cheek with the back of his hand and didn't seem to mind too much. She held him out at arm's length to look at him.

"Land sakes, Judge! Look at this boy. Dearie me!" "We're going to need to label these two boys to tell 'em apart, Sophie," Judge said, grinning. "I'm confused already."

Being part of a big family was something Johnny had to get used to, but he was so much like me that nobody had to get used to him. Right away he was just one of us, which was a good deal, if you think about it.

We trooped out to the pavilion where Daddy served drinks to the grown-ups. Just as I was starting to think I was goin' to starve, here came Jackson with a platter that had a huge pile of pork chops on it. Then came turnip greens, rice and gravy, biscuits, cold milk. The whole business was topped off later by pecan pie.

After supper was a great time to have fun, but we were too full to move. All us kids flopped out on the dark-red linoleum. Daddy leaned back in his chair.

"Lord, I'm full," he said.

I was thinking how purple the sky looked as it got dark, then I realized Uncle Todd was telling his angel story.

"...so there I was over the English Channel. This German plane had popped out of the clouds and got a shot at me before I managed to dive down into the fog that was hanging over the water. I found out later that one of his bullets hit the tail, but another bullet came through the cockpit and blasted my compass to little pieces. I flew in the fog as long as I dared, and when I came up the German was gone. I had clouds over me, fog down below, no compass and no idea which way England was. On top of all that, I had about a half-hour's worth of gas left, and...it was getting dark. I can tell you...I was doing some serious praying.

"I climbed as high as I could and flew in a big circle, hoping for a break in the fog. I was about out of gas. I figured I was in for a swim. It would have been a short one 'cause the English Channel will freeze you quick in December. Well, about then I saw this twinkling light way off to the right. Looked just like a bright star, but there weren't any stars out.

I remember I said "what the heck" out loud and headed for it.
I followed it, but I couldn't catch up to it. Then it seemed to go
down, so I did, too. I came to a break in the fog and dropped
down low, and there I was...a half-a-mile from the airfield. I
don't know who or what that light was, but I always thought
of it as my angel, and I can tell you, I've always felt mighty
kindly towards it...or him...or her...."

"I feel mighty kindly towards it, myself," Aunt Evelyn said,
and her voice sounded kind of husky.

Chapter Twenty-one

Johnny

WELL, I'D BEEN in my new home for about a week. Everybody had been real nice to me, and I was starting to feel at home, but I still hadn't got used to having a momma and a daddy. I still felt that pane of glass between me and them. I didn't feel that way about Will. Him and me was just like we had never been separated.

The morning Mr. Webb come in, Daddy picked him up in Montgomery and drove him to Birmingham. They got to the house just before lunch. After Mr. Webb got himself settled down in the guest room, Momma got us all some lemonade and we went on out to the pavilion. We was goin' to have some sandwiches there. Daddy was goin' to eat with us and then go back to the office.

Mr. Webb told me about Linc:

"He's looking a whole lot better, Johnny. He's pretty much got his strength back. The doctor said that he thought Linc had malaria, which was the kind of thing that could flare up from time to time and he gave him some-thing called quinine to take if he got sick again. He got himself some pads of paper and some pencils in Savannah, and he's working hard on his writing."

"How's ol' Hooter?" I asked him.

"Fine. Linc said she was mopey for a while after you left, but she's OK."

Mr. Webb had found someone to build a cottage for Joe and Bessie Carter and to fix up the house that Linc was goin' to live in. The same man was also goin' to do repairs on the plantation house. Joe and Bessie was busy trying to get the old house clean and Linc was starting to do some work on the grounds.

The wedding was in three weeks and then the Webbs was planning to go to Italy on their honeymoon. After that they figured on moving to the plantation.

"You know," Mr. Webb said to Daddy, "that plantation house is too big for Bessie to take care of alone. She's young, and she's a good worker, but she's not goin' to be able to do the housework and the laundry and cook. She prefers housework to cooking, so now we're looking for a cook. It seems silly to have four people looking after just the two of us, but that old house is huge, and we hope to have a lot of guests. It'll just get too boring if we don't. Grace will go nuts if we don't have friends coming to stay. By the way, I hope youall will come stay with us."

"Thank you, Beau," Momma said, "we'd love to come." "So far, we haven't had much luck finding a cook for the plantation," Mr. Webb said. "None of the women we tried to hire wanted to move away from Savannah."

Daddy was thinking. He looked at me:

"You know, son, that Mrs. Barncastle, the woman Sarah Davis was working for, wasn't well at all. She may have died. It's possible Sarah needs a job."

"Isn't Sarah Davis the colored lady who took care of Johnny when he was with the Brashers?" Mr. Webb asked.

"That's right, Beau. Johnny says she's a good cook and, we know for a fact she's a nice person."

"We'd love to have somebody like her," Mr. Webb said.

"You think she might be available?"

"I don't know, Beau," Daddy said. "I can get in touch with her. If you want me to, I'll check and see if she needs a job. I don't have any idea if she'd be willing to live way out in the country in Georgia."

"I'd really appreciate that, Frank. You can tell her that I pay better than most folks."

"If Sarah was working for Mr. Webb," I said, "I could see her when me and Will go to visit Linc. I'd love to be able to see Sarah. When can we go visit Linc, Daddy?"

"Next summer, Johnny. You'll be in school 'til then."

That evening, before supper, Mr. Webb come out on the screen porch where me and Will was reading. He sat on the day bed I was on.

"Johnny," he said, "Linc told me about Bobby Scagg." "All of it?" I asked him.

"All of it."

"I'm goin' to tell Momma and Daddy what happened," I said. "They won't tell nobody."

"No, they won't," Mr. Webb said.

After supper, we was all sitting around on the pavilion. It was almost dark, and we was looking out into the night watching the heat lightning flickering in the distance. Daddy lit his pipe.

"You folks sure know how to live," Mr. Webb said. "I love your house, and I love this pavilion."

"Ain't it wonderful here?" I asked him. "I never thought I could live in a place like this." Momma reached over and patted my cheek.

"It's wonderful for us to have you, honey," she said. She turned to Mr. Webb.

"I don't know what we'd do without this pavilion. We live out here during the summer." The lightning was moving closer and the sky lit up.

"Did youall ever see ball lightning?" Mr. Webb asked us. "I saw it at the plantation once when I was a boy. A storm was brewing up, and the air must have been charged with electricity. The front door blew open and, before I could close it, this ball of electricity rolled through the door, into the front hall and into the library. I looked in and there it sat...on the desk. It kind of exploded with a pop and disappeared."

"I'd love to see that," Will said. "Is ball lightning dangerous?"

"I don't know," Mr. Webb said. "I wasn't fixin' to go over and grab it!" We sat for a while watching the lightning.

"I want to tell youall...what happened to me and Linc," I said. "You got to not tell nobody."

"Go ahead, son," Daddy said. "We won't tell anyone." Everybody waited while I figured out how to start.

First I told them 'bout Hepburn and that Linc called him "the garbage man." Then I went on and told 'em 'bout Linc's dream. While I was getting into the story, I watched

Momma's eyes getting wider and wider. When I got to the part about Bobby Scagg coming in the boat to burn Linc's house, I saw Momma look at Daddy wide-eyed. She grabbed his arm with both hands and hung on.

"...So, there was light from the fire, see, and we seen these ripples movin' down the creek. I grabbed ahold of Linc, but I couldn't hardly talk. Linc said...'the garbage man took him'...."

"My God!" Momma said. "What an awful thing for a boy to see."

"Yes'm,' Johnny said. "It was awful, but...there was some way it seemed right. It weren't as awful as waitin' for that Bobby Scagg to come after us. When the garbage man took him, it put an end to that waitin'. Me and Linc was mighty relieved. The next day we danced around like a couple of crazy folks. Linc said that mean people sometimes finish themselves off."

"It's true," Mr. Webb said, "they destroy themselves, but they can do a whole lot of hurt before they get around to it."

I told 'em the rest of the story about getting rid of the boat and about Linc getting sick. When I finished, Momma told me to get up on the swing with her, and she put her arm aroun' me.

"That's some story, sweetie," she said. Daddy said:

"You and Linc packed a whole lot of stuff into that time in the swamp, didn't you, son."

"Yes, sir, I reckon we did," I told him.

"Beau," Daddy said, "Allie and I have been talking about what an unusually fine man Linc is. Where do you suppose his kind of fine character comes from?"

"Partly up-bringing, I suppose," Mr. Webb said, "but

somehow I think a lot of it is in the blood. Linc's father had the same kind of quality." Then he told them how Linc's daddy had helped the Webb family after the war.

"...when that Klan trash killed Josh Fraiser, it broke my father's heart. He started wearing a pistol. He told me later that he would have shot somebody if he could have found out who did that murder. You know...in a way, what happened to Bobby Scagg pays for that murder."

"That's what Linc said, too," I told him. "I think he feels more peaceful now about what happened to his daddy." We sat there in the candlelight, thinking and watching the lightning, and, then, Daddy said something wonderful to me:

"Son," he said, "your momma and I have been wanting to

do something for Linc. We decided it would be a good idea to buy him a motor. I talked to Mr. Webb about it this morning. He said a small Evinrude outboard motor would be just right for Linc's boat. Mr. Webb knows where he can get one in Savannah. We're goin' to give him the money for it, and when he goes back to the plantation, he'll take it to Linc." I jumped up.

"Oh, man!" I said. "That's great! Thanks for doing that! That's so great!" I gave 'em both a hug.

There was something about Momma and Daddy doing that for Linc that connected everything up. They know'd I loved Linc. When they bought him that motor, I believe they done it for me as much as Linc. It was right then that Momma and Daddy really started to feel like my folks. That pane of glass between them and me just went away. I felt years of being lonesome lifting up off of me. I took a deep breath and let it out.

I was home!

Chapter Twenty-two

Will

SUMMER SLID on out. The weather got cooler and the leaves began to turn.

September the third, school started. We hated to lose our summer freedom, but there was something kind of exciting about starting a new school year.

The week after Mr. Webb left, Daddy found out that Sarah Davis did need a job. Mrs. Barncastle had not died, but she had gotten too sick to live alone and had gone to live with her daughter. Sarah was taking some time off before she tried to find another job. When she heard about the job with Mr. Webb, she was doubtful about moving so far, but her daughter was getting married and needed a house. Daddy told her that Bessie and Joe were nice folks, but what really decided her was when she heard how Linc had taken care of Johnny, and that Johnny and me were goin' to be visiting Linc in the summer. Sarah knew that she would get to see Johnny from time to time if she was working for Mr. Webb, and that made up her mind. She decided to let her daughter live in her house and go to Georgia to try out the job with Mr. Webb.

When Daddy got back to Birmingham, he called Mr. Webb to arrange the whole business. Before Daddy hung up, Mr. Webb told Daddy that Linc was as excited as a kid when he had got that motor. Linc had asked Mr. Webb to thank Momma and Daddy for the motor and said that when his writing got better he would write them a letter.

Johnny slipped into my class at Mountain Brook School like goose grease. It was the same story at school that it had been with the family. Nobody had to get used to Johnny. Right off the bat, my friends were his friends...Tommy Varner, Scooter Wilks, Jimmy Rainwater, whom we called Pud for "puddle," and, of course, Reginald Marcellus Jenkins, who, for some reason, preferred to be called "Butch."

Daddy usually dropped us at school on his way to the office. Sometimes, we'd go home with Pud Rainwater after school and play football in his back yard.

Momma would usually pick us up after school or at Pud's house at five o'clock. If she couldn't, Jackson would come for us in the station wagon.

On weekends, we would usually have at least one of our friends over to spend one or two nights. Once in a while, Momma would let us have a spend-the-night party with several friends at once. We'd stay up most of the night, talking, telling ghost stories, wrestling, and sneaking around the house and yard. I'm sure we kept Momma and Daddy awake most of the night, and we messed up the house pretty good, too. Even after we cleaned up the mess the next morning, the house didn't look so good, and Momma and Jackson would have to put it back together.

One Friday about three weeks after school started, we had Pud over to spend the night. Daddy said we were all goin' to the movies at the Strand. It was a double feature; a movie called *A Sherlock Holmes Mystery* with Basil Rathbone and Nigel Bruce and one called *The Spider Woman* with Mary Gordon. We were very excited even though it meant we all had to put on shoes. We had cold ham, potato salad, and beaten biscuits for an early supper; got our shoes on; and all piled in Daddy's car.

I think those were the best movies I ever saw. We went in the movie theater at about seven and didn't get home 'til after eleven, but nobody but Daddy got sleepy. Daddy always sleeps through movies. He put his head back after the newsreel and slept through both features.

The next day, me and Johnny and Pud came up with a game we called Sherlock Holmes and the missing twin. Pud was Sherlock Holmes, and Johnny and I took turns being Dr. Watson who was looking for his missing twin. Whoever was playing the missing twin would go off somewhere but would leave clues written on little pieces of paper, like a treasure hunt. It was a fun game. The only trouble was that it was boring being the missing twin and waiting to be found. The second time I was the missing twin, I took a book with me so I could read while Holmes and Watson unraveled the clues I had left. I sat in the cave under the big boulder in the woods and read *Treasure Island* until I heard them coming.

"I say, old chap," I heard Pud say. "My deduction is that your stupid, ugly brother is hiding under that there rock over yonder."

"Remember, my dear Holmes," Johnny told him, "if you

insult my twin brother, you also insult me, and I, Dr. Watson, will knock a knot on your head!"

By October, fall had come for sure. We helped Jackson rake leaves into huge piles and, before we burned them, had a great time diving into them and burying Charlie in them. There was a bumper crop of acorns that year. Some places the acorns were three or four inches deep. It was kind of frustrating. It seemed like there ought to be something really fun to do with all those acorns, but we could never figure out what.

One Sunday afternoon, me and Johnny got in trouble. It was a rainy day, and we were stuck indoors. All our comic books had gotten stale. There was nothing good on the radio. I was rummaging around in a drawer where I kept my favorite things, hoping to find something interesting, when I came across a cement-coated cherry-bomb firecracker. I don't know who thought of it, probably me, but we got to wondering what it would be like to shoot it off in the toilet. Those cherry bombs had waterproof fuses. You could light one and throw it in the creek, and it would go off under two feet of water with a muffled "whumph!" I don't know what we thought would happen.

I guess we figured the water in the toilet would muffle the sound so Momma and Daddy wouldn't hear it, and we could get away with the experiment. We began to think how much more interesting it would be if we flushed it, but for some reason, we decided not to do that. Well, I lit the fuse and dropped the cherry bomb in the toilet, and we ran into our bedroom. There was a terrific bang. Momma and Daddy had been in the library. Before we knew it, they were in our bedroom asking frantically what in the world had happened. We looked in the bathroom and water was spurting up on the ceiling. There wasn't a piece of toilet bowl left that was bigger than a hen's egg. Our folks couldn't believe it. We were protesting that we never knew it would blow the toilet to smithereens. Momma said we could have been hurt by those flying pieces of toilet. We said it wasn't dangerous because we had run out of the bathroom. Daddy, who had shut off the valve to stop the water from spurting, was just standing there shaking his head.

"If you didn't believe it would blow the toilet to pieces, why did you run out of the bathroom?" Daddy wanted to know. We couldn't think of a good answer to that one.

"What do we do about this, Allie?" Daddy said. "If it was Butch or Pud, we could send 'em home, but both of these characters are already home."

"Just a minute, Frank," Momma said. She left and came back with two pads of legal paper.

"Johnny, you stay here, and Will you go in the guest room. I don't want to see you two characters until supper, and I want you to do some writing. See what it says on these pads?" It said: I won't ever do anything this dumb again.

"Yes'm," we told her.

"I want each of you to write that one hundred times, please," Momma said.

"I'm goin' to call the plumber," Daddy said.

I think it was right then that Johnny knew for sure he wasn't ever goin' to get whipped anymore. If doing something that dumb wouldn't get us whipped, nothing would. Anyway, blowing up the toilet loosened things up for Johnny. After that, he didn't have any more problem with being too good.

⌒⌒

Things were looking mighty glum that evening when we came to the dinner table. Momma and Daddy were sitting there looking real serious.

"I sure am sorry we blew up the toilet," I said. "Me, too," Johnny said.

Momma and Daddy looked at each other and started to laugh.

"Live and learn, you little stinkers. Live and learn," Daddy said.

"At least we got a good story out of this," Momma said. "I can't wait to tell Todd!"

Chapter Twenty-three

Johnny

MONDAY NIGHT THE ROOF fell in. We was all sitting around the library listening to the "Lux Radio Theater" when the phone rang. Momma answered the phone and we were watching her. She said:

"Hello. Who? Oh, hello, Aaron..." she listened, then she turned white.

"Oh, no!" she gasped.

"What's the matter, honey?" Daddy went over to the phone.

"It's Mr. Steiner, in Columbia. He said Mrs. Brasher has changed her mind and is goin' to try to get custody of Johnny."

That put us in shock. Daddy got on the phone.

"Aaron, how in the world can the judge allow such a thing?" He listened and then said: "Hold on a minute," and turned to us.

"Mr. Steiner said that since no formal action has been taken, Mrs. Brasher is entitled to change her mind. He said that her lawyer told the judge that she had felt intimidated by what important, big-city folks we were, but that she had been praying about it and had decided that it was her Christian duty to her dead sister to bring up Johnny."

Lord! I was back in the pits again, only worse than before. Daddy was still talking to Mr. Steiner, but I quit listening. I had got used to having a home and being part of a family who loved me, and now it looked like all that might be took away. I looked up at Momma and she tried to smile. She come over and sat next to me on the floor and put her arm around my shoulders.

"We'll work it out, honey," she said. "We've got to. We're not goin' to let you go now."

～～～

There ain't no way I can tell you how bad it was waiting to go back and have that hearing. None of us ate much or got much sleep after that phone call from Mr. Steiner. Thank heavens for school. We went to school Tuesday and Wednesday and that helped to pass the time. All of us got more and more worried, though.

Thursday morning just before we were goin' to leave for the station to catch the train to Columbia, Mr. Steiner called again.

When Daddy hung up, he told us that Mr. Steiner said he had lined up Sarah and my old teacher, Miss Brownlee to be witnesses at the hearing.

"Thank goodness Sarah hadn't already gone to Georgia," Momma said.

"Yeah, we need her," Daddy said.

It was a sorry-looking bunch of folks that got off that train in Columbia and checked into the Bethel hotel.

～～～

That night, when Will and me was in the double bed, Daddy told us goodnight and then Momma come in. I could tell she'd been crying. When she sat down on our bed, I reached out and patted her.

"Don't worry, Momma," I told her. "It's goin' to be all right."

"Thank you, honey," she said. She got her arms around both of us and hugged us like she would never turn lose.

After she left I said:

"Will, if that judge tries to make me go back to Aunt Min, I'm goin' to run off again. Remember, I told you that before? Well, I'm not kiddin'. I ain't stayin' with Aunt Min no more."

"I know you're not kidding," he said. "If it comes to you runnin' off again, let's you and me meet up at the Webb place. Linc would take us out in the swamp." We settled on that plan, but it weren't much comfort.

The next morning in the dining room none of us could eat more than a piece of toast. We had some milk, and Momma and Daddy had coffee. Daddy heaved a big sigh and pushed back from the table. The hearing wouldn't start 'til eleven. Three more hours to wait. We sat in the lobby and worried and fidgeted for what seemed like two weeks; then, we went to our same old benches in the courthouse square and worried and fidgeted for another week. Finally, Daddy told us it was time.

It was a hot day for October. In the courtroom, it was even worse…hot and stuffy. As we was goin' in the courtroom, Daddy pulled off his coat. I looked around. Mr. Steiner was already there.

There was benches like pews and two long tables with chairs behind them in front of the benches. Mr. Steiner come over and took us to our table, and we all set down. More waiting. I looked around and saw Uncle Joe and Aunt Min come in with their lawyer and Mrs. Spears. Mrs. Spears set on one of the benches and Uncle Joe and Aunt Min and their lawyer set at the other table.

"Johnny, do you know who that lady is?" Mr. Steiner asked me.

"Yes, sir, that's Mrs. Spears. She teaches Sunday school at Uncle Joe's church."

I turned around and saw Sarah in the back of the courtroom and my teacher, Miss Brownlee, right behind us. I waved at both of them and they waved back.

We waited in that hot courtroom. I looked around at the faded yellow walls and grimy windows. It was a place that had seen a heap of troubles. A man in uniform with sweat stains under his arms went over and turned on a ceiling fan. It didn't move much air, but every time the blade went around it made a noise. "Click." We set there and sweated and listened to that fan clicking: "Click…Click…Click." It begun to get on my nerves. At last the judge come in and the man in uniform told us to get up, and we did. He said:

"The Third Circuit Court of Maury County is now in session, Judge Thomas J. King presiding. Be seated."

The judge looked down at us like he wished we wasn't there and mopped his face with a handkerchief. Then he started talking and went over what was goin' to happen and asked the lawyers for "opening remarks" and Mr. Steiner said:

"Your Honor, we intend to show that the boy, Johnny Brasher, was placed in a home where he was mistreated by his aunt, Minnie Brasher. We believe that he should not have been separated from his twin brother, Will, and that it will be in the best interests of the boy, Johnny, that he not return to the Brasher's home. And, finally, we ask that permanent custody be awarded to the petitioners, Mr. and Mrs. Frank Jennison, the adoptive parents of Johnny's twin brother, Will."

Next, the other lawyer got up and said:

"Your Honor, we are goin' to show that The Brashers gave the boy, Johnny, a good home; that the boy was a difficult child, and that he received only the necessary discipline consistent with improving his character so that he would grow up to be a useful member of society. I want to point out that the boy is the blood kin of Minnie Brasher, which makes it natural for him to remain in her care. We feel it would be grossly unfair to take a child away from somebody who has invested years of her life in raising him."

Mr. Steiner asked Sarah to take the stand. She told how it was at Aunt Min's, and she didn't leave nothing out. She even told about hearing Aunt Min say she didn't want me. After she finished, Mr. Slade got to ask her some questions.

"Mrs. Davis," he said, "do you often hide behind doors and listen to other people's private conversations?"

"Objection!" Mr. Steiner hollered. "Mrs. Davis was not hiding behind the door."

"Sustained," said the judge.

"Well, then, do you often listen in on other people's personal conversations?"

"I didn't want to bus' in right in the middle..." "Answer the question, Mrs. Davis! Do you often listen in on private conversations?" "No, suh."

"Is it true that you were fired without references from your employment with the Brashers for not following orders?"

"Yes, suh, but I..."

"That you deliberately undermined Mrs. Brasher's discipline?"

"No, suh, I..."

"Isn't it true that the reason Johnny was such an unruly boy is because you consistently undermined Mrs. Brasher's discipline?"

"No, suh, I..." Mr. Steiner jumped up.

"Objection! That calls for a conclusion from the witness."

"Sustained."

"That's all, Mrs. Davis."

Mr. Steiner was still on his feet and he spoke to Sarah again: "Mrs. Davis, why did you get fired?"

"Miz Brasher sent Johnny to bed without no supper, but she done it too much. He was puny. I was 'fraid he would starve or get sick. A growin' boy need food an' I used to give it to him. Mrs. Brasher foun' out 'bout me givin' Johnny food. She said I was a useless nigger, an' she fire me."

"Thank you, Mrs. Davis." Mr. Steiner sat down and Sarah started to get up.

"Just a minute please, Mrs. Davis," Mr. Slade said. "Did the boy starve, Mrs. Davis?"

"No, suh, I..."

"Did you think as a colored employee it was your place to judge your white employer's actions in disciplining her ward?" Mr. Steiner was up again.

"Objection, Your Honor! Race has nothing to do with this."

"I'll change the question," Mr. Slade said. "Mrs. Davis, do you think it is an employee's place to judge the actions of an employer?"

"No, suh," Sarah said, looking miserable. They let her get down and go to the back of the courtroom. I got up to go back with her and give her a hug, but Mr. Steiner put his hand on my shoulder and made me sit down.

Mr. Steiner asked Miss Brownlee to get up on the stand. They made her swear to tell the truth, and then Mr. Steiner started to ask her questions:

"Miss Brownlee, were you worried about the condition of your pupil Johnny Brasher?"

"Yes, sir, I was."

"Please, tell the court about his condition."

"He was skinny and usually dirty. On cold days he wasn't dressed warmly enough and lots of days his legs were all marked up."

"Marked how?"

"Red welts and stripes from switching."

"Objection!" Mr. Slade hollered. "The witness is giving her opinion."

"Sustained," the judge said.

"Did you voice these concerns to anybody?"

"Yes, sir. I went to see Mrs. Brasher and told her I was worried about Johnny's condition."

"Then what happened?"

"She asked me to explain, and I told her that I didn't think Johnny was getting enough to eat, that he was not adequately dressed when it was cold, and that he was getting whipped too much."

"What happened then, Miss Brownlee?"

"She became very angry, almost insanely angry. She cursed me and called me bad things."

"What bad things?"

"She said I was 'a meddling bitch.' She told me to mind my own business and get out of her house. Her eyes were bugging out. She was practically foaming at the mouth. It was frightening."

"What did you do, Miss Brownlee?" "I left as quickly as I could."

"Thank you, Miss Brownlee. Your witness," Mr. Steiner said.

Mr. Slade got up. "Miss Brownlee, did you ever whip an unruly student?"

"Yes, but . . ."

"In fact, Miss Brownlee, did you ever have a student who was bad enough to require repeated whippings?"

"Yes, but Johnny wasn't..."

"Thank you, Miss Brownlee." Mr. Steiner got up.

"Miss Brownlee," he said, "was Johnny Brasher a difficult child to discipline?"

"No, sir. He didn't need any discipline. When I corrected him, no matter how gentle I was, he looked scared."

"Thank you, Miss Brownlee. You're excused. I'd like to call Mrs. Brasher to the stand." After Aunt Min was swore in, Mr. Steiner said:

"Mrs. Brasher, was Johnny a good boy when he was in your care?" He pointed at me, but Aunt Min wouldn't look. She stared straight ahead.

"No, sir. He was bad. Broke things, messed up, didn't do his chores right...He was dirty, and he was defiant."

"Did you find Johnny a difficult boy to discipline?"

"I couldn't get nowhere with him. It was that nigra, that Sarah. She undercut everything I done."

"You whipped the boy?"

"I switched him when he was bad. He was defiant. He wouldn't cry. He'd just clamp his mouth shut and stare off in space. After I switched him, he'd go back to the kitchen. I reckon that Sarah would tell him how good he was. I know that when I sent him to bed without supper, that nigra would sneak him food behind my back."

"Mrs. Brasher, how often did you send Johnny to bed with no supper?"

"Not often. Only when he was bad." "So he wasn't bad often, then."

"He was bad all the time."

"So you sent him to bed with no supper all the time?" Aunt Min was starting to grind her teeth. You could see her jaw muscles bunching up.

"Objection, Your Honor! The witness has already answered the question."

"Sustained," the judge said. "Move on, Mr. Steiner." "Mrs. Brasher, if Johnny is such a difficult child, why do you want to retain custody?"

"I don't see why some rich, city folks should come up here and take away my own sister's boy after I've had him fer so long. I have a Christian duty to my dead sister. Without that nigra interferin', I believe I can bring up that boy to be a God-fearin' man."

"He'll certainly fear you, Mrs. Brasher," Mr. Steiner said.

"Objection!"

"Sustained. No more remarks like that, Mr. Steiner." "Sorry, Your Honor."

"Mrs. Brasher, did you leave Johnny alone for three days?"

"We went to a revival in Columbia. The boy had plenty of food. All he had to do was feed the animals." "Did you leave him alone for three days?" "Yes. He was old enough to see to himself."

"Mrs. Brasher, when Johnny ran away, did you report him missing?"

"No. I figured he'd come back."

"Isn't it true that Johnny had been gone for close to a week and that you still hadn't reported him missing."

"He used to go off sometimes. I thought he would be back."

"Did he leave a note?" Mr. Steiner asked her. "He wrote somethin'."

"What did he write?"

"I don't rightly remember. Somethin' about he was goin' off for a spell."

"Did you love the boy, Mrs. Brasher?"

"'Course I did. That's why I punished him when he's bad."

"I see. Whipping is your way of expressing love?" "Objection!"

"Mr. Steiner!" Judge King said.

"No further questions, Your Honor."

Aunt Min was looking mighty pinched around the lips. Mr. Slade got up and went over to question her. She had started to grind her teeth, and there was a kind of wild look in her eyes. Mr. Slade looked at her nervously.

"No questions," he said and took Aunt Min back to her seat at the table.

Daddy was the next person who got up on the stand. Mr. Steiner asked him a lot of questions about himself and his work until the judge finally said:

"The court accepts the fact that Mr. Jennison is a respected member of his community. Please get on with it, Mr. Steiner."

"Yes, Your Honor. Mr. Jennison, why do you and Mrs. Jennison want custody of Johnny?"

"Well, sir, I believe Mrs. Brasher is mentally unbalanced, and that she mistreated Johnny."

"What makes you believe that she mistreated the boy, sir?"

"We know from Sarah Davis and from what Johnny has told us that Mrs. Brasher was consistently mean to the boy to the point of cruelty. Miss Brownlee just said that his legs were always marked up."

"What gives you the impression that Mrs. Brasher is mentally unbalanced?"

"When I questioned Mrs. Brasher about her and Mr. Brasher leaving Johnny alone for three days, and about them not reporting him missing, she behaved very strangely."

"How did she behave, Mr. Jennison?"

"She began to curse and threaten me and to rant and rave like a madwoman. Ever since then and since we found out how she treated him, we have felt that Mrs. Brasher was not fit to bring up the boy."

"Is there any other reason why you and your wife want custody over the boy, Mr. Jennison?"

"We don't feel the twins should be separated. We have believed this all along. Back when Johnny and Will's parents were killed, we tried to adopt them both, but Mrs. Brasher insisted on taking Johnny, so the boys were separated. Now that Johnny and Will are back together, the bond between them is quite apparent. It would be wrong to separate them again." Mr. Steiner thanked him, and Mr. Slade got up to ask questions.

"Mr. Jennison, you're not a psychiatrist, or any kind of

medical specialist in mental illness are you?" "No, sir, I'm not."

"Yet you consider yourself competent to judge someone 'mentally unbalanced'?"

"Yes, sir, I do. I am quite sure that the term 'mentally unbalanced' is not a medical term. Lay people, yourself included, make judgments about people's 'mental balance' all the time." Mr. Slade was caught by this answer. He coughed and walked around the courtroom to gain time.

"And you and your wife would take a child away from a loving aunt, who has loved him since he was two years old?"

"I don't accept the premise of your question. This particular woman is not loving and should not have control over a child."

"You're an important, big-city businessman, Mr. Jennison, used to telling folks what to do. Do you think you can come to our little town and have everybody jump to do what you say?"

"Mr. Slade, if I thought that, I wouldn't be so worried. I'm worried sick about this business. We've already lost custody over Johnny once. I'm scared to death it could happen again."

"You don't look like a man who would scare easily, Mr. Jennison. What exactly are you scared of?"

"I'm scared of what will happen to Johnny if we lose," he said. "We love the boy."

"That's very sentimental, Mr. Jennison, but you've only known the boy for a matter of weeks."

"Johnny is our son's identical twin, Mr. Slade. It didn't take us five minutes to start to love him."

Mrs. Spears was the only witness Mr. Slade called. She got up there and told the judge what a good, Christian woman Aunt Min was, and she said she know'd her well; but, when Mr. Steiner questioned her, she admitted that she had only seen Mrs. Brasher at church doin's.

The judge asked the two lawyers to sum up, and each one of 'em talked for a few minutes, goin' over what had already been said at the hearings. Both of them talked about some other cases. It seemed like they thought legal stuff other judges had done would help Judge King make up his mind. They went on quite a while about all that. Finally the judge started to talk:

"Since these two boys have already been separated for a number of years, I don't consider their separation to be the overriding issue in this case. The only way I would consider taking a child away from a blood relation who'd had custody for so long would be if gross negligence or mistreatment had been conclusively proved. I may be old-fashioned, but I am not prepared to take the word of a nigra servant against a white woman who is known to be a respected member of her community and a pillar of her church...."

I was feeling lower and lower. There was a hollow, sick feeling in the bottom of my stomach. I looked at Momma. She was pale and looked scared. She was sitting between Will and me, and when I looked at her, she reached and got my hand in her left hand and Will's in her right. She was holding on tight.

"...therefore, it is my ruling that..."

"Your Honor!" Everybody turned to look. It was Uncle Joe standing up behind the table. "I got to say something."

"Does it have a direct bearing on this hearing, Mr. Brasher?

"Yes, sir, it does." Mr. Slade jumped up. "Objection! Your Honor, I...

"Mr. Slade, the court will hear Mr. Brasher. He is directly involved in this matter. Bailiff, swear Mr. Brasher." Uncle Joe took the oath, and then he turned to the judge.

"Your Honor, my wife ain't no blood kin to the boy Johnny."

"What do you mean, sir?" the judge asked him.

"Minnie herself was a foundling."

The courtroom was dead quiet except for the clicking of that fan. We sat there in the steamy heat. A fly lit on our table. I looked at Aunt Min. She was staring at Uncle Joe like she wanted to kill him.

"Minnie never told nobody this but me, but she was took in by Johnny's mother's folks, the Lawsons, when she was just a baby. She didn't even have no name. Nobody know'd whose child she was. She was found when she was about a week old, wrapped up in rags in a park in Columbus, Georgia. Sometime after that the Lawsons moved to Columbia. They named the baby Minnie and raised her as their own, as Betsy Lawson's sister. Betsy Lawson married Peter Hance, and they was the twins' parents. My wife ain't no blood kin to either one of them boys." Everybody was stunned. I looked at Aunt Min and her eyes was bugging out and a line of spit was coming out of one corner of her mouth.

"One more thing, Your Honor. That Sarah Davis told the truth. My wife didn't feed that boy enough, and she whipped him too hard and too much fer makin' mistakes. He weren't bad, just careless like most boys. It hurt me to see him whipped so. I am ashamed to say I didn't stop it."

Aunt Min stood up and started towards Uncle Joe like she was in some kind of a trance. She held her hands out in front of her with her thumbs and fingers hooked into claws. She staggered almost to the witness chair and then her hands and arms fell limp to her sides. Nobody else in the courtroom moved. It was like we was all hypnotized by what was happening.

"Bastard!" She hissed, "I'll…kill…you!" and then this high, whining scream come out of her, and her hands come back up, and she lunged at Uncle Joe trying to claw his eyes. The judge was banging his hammer and calling for order. The man in uniform jumped up and headed towards the witness chair, but before he could get there, Uncle Joe was on his feet.

"Shut up, Minnie!" he bellowed in his best hell-fire voice. "You ain't goin' to do this to me no more!" Uncle Joe grabbed both her wrists, got 'em pinned in his big left hand and drew back his right hand and slapped her open-handed. Her knees sagged, and her eyes went glassy. Uncle Joe picked her up and carried her to a bench and laid her on it. She pulled her knees up, covered her face with her hands and started to cry like I ain't never heard no one cry. Uncle Joe knelt down by the bench and patted her.

"It's all right, Min. It's all right..." he said over and over again.

After everything calmed down, I remember the judge saying that in the light of what he had just found out, he was awarding custody to the Jennisons. Me and Will was hugging each other. I saw Uncle Joe leading Aunt Min out of the courtroom. She was all hunched over like an old, old lady. I looked up at the Jennisons.

They sat down and put their arms around me and Will. "Thank God, that's over!" Daddy said.

"I want to see Sarah," I said.

Chapter Twenty-four

Will

WELL, WE GOT BACK from Tennessee. At last, Johnny was home for good, and I was, too. I had had a wonderful life with Momma and Daddy, but without Johnny there, it hadn't felt all the way like home. Now I knew I was where I belonged. Johnny and I had found each other, and we were home.

A few days after the hearing, Johnny got a letter from Uncle Joe. It said:

Dear Johnny,

> *Here is a picture of your folks. I thought you and Will would like to have it. I am sorry I didn't look after you better. You are a good boy and didn't deserve to be treated so hard.*

Love, Uncle Joe

The picture showed our folks standing in front of a Model A Ford. Our mother was pretty and blond and our dad was tall with freckles. Even though the picture was black and white you could tell he had red hair like ours. That picture was a big help to us.

One day several weeks after the hearing Daddy came

home grinning. He had an envelope in his hand. Me and Johnny had just come in from the woods where we had been exploring with Charlie. Daddy asked me to get Jenny May, and Jackson and he went to find Momma. When we were all in the library, Daddy said:

"I've got a surprise. A present for all of us." He opened the envelope and took out some papers.

"These are the final adoption papers," he told us. "Johnny,…" he looked at me, and I pointed at Johnny, "is now Johnny Jennison!" We all cheered and Momma came over and hugged me and Johnny at the same time. Daddy said:

"I'm not much of a church-goin' man, but when you feel as grateful as I do, it's time to say so." He smiled and looked up.

"Thank you, Lord!" he said.

"Amen!" said Momma and Jenny May and Jackson. Johnny and me chimed in.

"Amen!

Chapter Twenty-five

Johnny

As TIME WENT by, I was finding out that I didn't remember the bad times as well as the good times. All them years with Aunt Min was fading out like a bad dream. The time with Linc, though, was as clear as crystal. I never forgot it. Not none of it.

So many good folks had helped me. Sarah and Linc saved my life, and Momma and Daddy and Will gave me a whole new life. "Lucky" don't begin to cover it.

A week after the adoption papers come through, I got a letter from Linc. There was lots of mistakes in it, but I could read it fine. It said:

Deer Johnny

    This here gon' be Lincs furst leter. I stil cant spel worth nuthin but thanks to you Johnny – I can rite and Bessie and Sara say I be gettin beter. I rote yo folks a letter about the motor they got me. It is a joy to have it when my shoulders are feeling stif. Me and Sarah talks about you boys alots. Sara be a good harted lady and can she cook. Linc dont look out – he be to fat to roe a boat. Got to watch out fo' Hooter to. She been eatin kichen skraps and like em a hole lot beter than pig food. Mr. Webb say you boys comin fo' a month in july. Sara say youall got to stay at the house some so she get to see you but soon as I can – I gon take you boys to my house up in that swamp. We gon catch some big ole bass and Linc gon make you a cat fish stu with some corn cakes. I been up in the swamp some – Johnny and I be glad I ain't seen that Hepburn no more. I think he gon. Hooter an me both miss you – Johnny. Sara send her love to you boys – and I does to.

                               Your friend, Linc

After I got that letter, I wrote back to Linc. It was the first letter I ever wrote, too, and it took me some time to write it....

Dear Linc,

    It was wonderful to get your letter. You can sure write a whole lots now.

    I know how good a cook Sarah is, but I just can't picture you fat. I know you are kidding me about that.

    I been having a happy time with Momma and Daddy and Will. It is great to have a family. You said they would be my family and they are. Being back with Will is so good.

I don't get lonesome no more except for you and Sarah because you and Sarah are my best friends. I am so glad we are goin' to see youall next summer. I can't wait to show Will what it's like to live in the swamp. He has showed me so much. I want to show him some stuff.

Will and me have a lots of fun but not as much as you and me had. Give a big hug to Hooter and give my love to Sarah and say hello to Mr. Webb for me and Will.

Love, Johnny

About the Author

 I live on Mercer Island, Washington, near Seattle, with my wife Jill, my filmmaker son Ben, who is now a weekend visitor, and three dogs; Sunshine, Piccolo, and Chloe. My daughter April, who is currently making a documentary film, lives nearby in Seattle, and my first son, Colby, a filmmaker, lives in New Orleans. (I have to wonder if a gene for filmmaking runs in my family!)

At the age of seventy-seven, I now pursue my two passions: writing and jazz guitar.

I was born and raised outside of Birmingham, Alabama. You can take a Southerner out of the South, but you can't take the South out of a Southerner!

As a boy I had the good fortune of growing up with the space and freedom to be outside, have adventures, explore, and get into trouble. A boy's purpose in life is to play, and the tantalizing possibility of getting into trouble added spice to that purpose.

I was also blessed with a rich heritage of storytelling from the members of my wonderful, extended Southern family. I share some of my family stories in the Blackwater Novels.

My boyhood in the South and my college years at the University of Alabama also gave me first-hand experience of the good people of both races coming together with love to help each other and to confront racial hatred.

I am grateful to my Southern past for giving me the rich experiences to draw on in writing the Blackwater Novels. I consider these books to be parables on how to live. This may explain why some things work out better in the novels than they do in real life.

— Allen Johnson Jr.

Answering the Question
I Am Asked Most Often

I am frequently asked how much of a novel is autobiographical.
The following passages from *Fun! a boyhood*—a memoir about
my boyhood—will show how I take atmosphere, events, character
names and settings from my own boyhood and mix them in with
fictional stuff to write the Blackwater Novels. Incidentally, most of
the family stories that are told in these books are true.

MY GRANDPARENTS' HOME AND THE PAVILION
(The Alabama setting for the Blackwater Novels)

After a mile of dusty dirt road that ran past the pasture, you would
come to my grandparents' weathered, paved drive. It climbed past
a sweeping, informal lawn to the rambling, ivy-covered, sandstone house. Their home was one of those houses that looked like
it had grown into the Southern countryside. In back of the house,
overlooking the valley, was the pavilion: a porch-like structure
with a wood-shingled roof, a dark red linoleum floor, porch furniture, a chain-suspended porch swing, and a painted giraffe from a
carousel. The pavilion was the scene of family gatherings on long
summer evenings.

SOUTHERN FOOD

My grandfather loved to eat and ate like a European, piling up
savory combinations of Southern cooking on the back of his fork
which he kept in his left hand. My grandparents had a cook named
Maggie Maccadory, a birdlike, tiny black woman who couldn't have
weighed a hundred pounds. Maggie was an artist who up until

about 1940 still cooked on a wood stove. In the tradition of most Southern cooks, most vegetables were overcooked with salt pork ("side meat"), and meats were well-done and seasoned with lots of pepper, but somehow after several home-grown vegetables had appeared, with corn pudding, fried chicken, tomatoes and onions in oil and vinegar, and homemade biscuits with country butter, my plate would resemble a work of art.

BLOWING UP THE TOILET

Cherry bombs were cement-covered firecrackers which packed the punch of a small stick of dynamite and which, unfortunately, could be set off under water. I say "unfortunately" because this fact led John Seals and me to set one off in my toilet. The only question at that time was whether or not to flush it. We didn't. There was no piece of toilet bowl left that was bigger than a hen's egg. Good thing we didn't flush. A blasted toilet bowl was better than a burst pipe in the walls.

There are numerous other experiences in my boyhood that I use in the Blackwater Novels. Many are in my memoir, *Fun! A boyhood*. As I have said elsewhere, I am a pretty good writer but was a total genius at being a boy.

— Allen Johnson Jr.

☙Blackwater Novels☙

The Blackwater Novels are set in the 1930s along the Blackwater River and Blackwater Swamp, near the fictional town of Turpentine, Georgia, and in the countryside near Birmingham, Alabama.

Explore the magic and mystery of nature . . . hear the critters in the swamp, sleep in a treehouse, find a hidden grave, and sleep on an island by the embers of a campfire. Get in trouble with the twins when they shoot green tomatoes in a giant slingshot and blow up a toilet with a cherry bomb. Join Linc, Sheriff Clyde and Dr. Mason when they confront the poisonous nest of snakes called the Ku Klux Klan, and Henry Granger's evil presence in the Dead House.

My Brother's Story

Identical twins Johnny and Will are orphaned and separated as toddlers. When he grows into boyhood, Johnny runs away and is sheltered by Linc, a reclusive black man who lives deep in the Blackwater Swamp. *My Brother's Story* tells of the twins' adventures as they struggle to reunite.

The Dead House

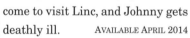

Rad Fox, a boy who lives on the Blackwater River, and family friend Dr. Jordan Mason discover an evil presence at the old Granger House. Johnny and Will come to visit Linc, and Johnny gets deathly ill.   AVAILABLE APRIL 2014

A Nest of Snakes

While sleeping in their treehouse, the twins overhear a plot. At the Blackwater River they join Rad Fox to help Linc and Sheriff Clyde who are in danger from the Ku Klux Klan. Once again, good people join together to confront racial hatred.   AVAILABLE JULY 2014

Order at **blackwaternovels.com**
Available in hardcover and ebook